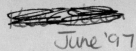

'What are you going to do about finding a father for your baby?'

'I'm thinking of going down to Bramdale Clinic to discuss the possibilities of artificial insemination,' Jenni replied in a rush, anxious to get the idea over to him. She didn't want him to think that she was looking around for a suitable man. . .but then again. . .

That idea had certain advantages. And disadvantages too!

'There could be a simpler solution,' Carl said carefully.

She took a deep breath. 'Which is?'

'Well. . .'

GW00401838

Kids. . .one of life's joys, one of life's treasures.

Kisses. . .of warmth, kisses of passion, kisses from mothers and kisses from lovers.

In *Kids & Kisses*. . .every story has it all.

Margaret Barker pursued a variety of interesting careers before she became a full-time author. Besides holding a degree in French and Linguistics, she is a Licentiate of the Royal Academy of Music, a State Registered Nurse and a qualified teacher. Happily married, she has two sons, a daughter and an increasing number of grandchildren. She lives with her husband in a sixteenth-century thatched house near the East Anglian coast.

Recent titles by the same author:

INTIMATE PRESCRIPTION
LOVED AND LOST

I'D LOVE
A BABY!

BY
MARGARET BARKER

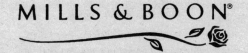

MILLS & BOON®

*MILLS & BOON and MILLS & BOON with the Rose Device
are registered trademarks of the publisher.*

*First published in Great Britain 1997
Harlequin Mills & Boon Limited,
Eton House, 18-24 Paradise Road, Richmond, Surrey TW9 1SR*

© Margaret Barker 1997

ISBN 0 263 80209 4

*Set in Times 10 on 11½ pt. by
Rowland Phototypesetting Limited
Bury St Edmunds, Suffolk*

03-9708-45464-D

*Printed and bound in Great Britain
by Mackays of Chatham PLC, Chatham*

CHAPTER ONE

'So, what do you make of him, Jenni?'

'Who?'

'The new senior registrar, of course! Everybody's talking about him.'

Staff Nurse Rona Phillips gave a sigh of exasperation. 'Surely you haven't failed to notice that he's the most gorgeous. . .'

'Honestly, Rona! You seem to think everybody's man-mad, like yourself. I have to work on my ward with the man more than you do so I intend to keep him in his place.'

Jenni pushed long strands of blonde hair away from her eyes as she finished speaking, wishing that she could escape the endless hospital gossip. She was beginning to regret having accepted a lift from the hospital with Rona, but the staff nurse had seemed so keen to show Jenni her new car that she hadn't liked to disappoint her.

Rain was pouring down in relentless sheets outside the porch of Cragdale Church. It seemed as if the entire medical staff of Moortown General Hospital was gathered inside. Jenni had already removed the frothy piece of net that masqueraded as a designer hat and stuffed it in her shoulder-bag. Her sheer tights were splattered with muddy rainwater from the hurried flight up the path, and as for the new, stone-coloured suit. . .! That would definitely have to go to the cleaners next week.

The porch was crammed with guests who wanted to

catch a first glimpse of the bride, before taking their
seats in the already overflowing pews.

'Here she comes!'

Jenni craned her neck. A white, mud-spattered Rolls
Royce was pulling up outside the lych-gate. Behind it
a sleek, silver coupé ground to a halt, the driver's door
opening immediately to allow a tall, athletic figure to
spring out.

From the depths of the bridal car the bride's father
was struggling to unfold an umbrella whilst, at the same
time, helping his daughter to alight. Yards of precious
lace seemed destined to be sacrificed to the elements.

The tall, dark-haired man from the car behind was
opening an enormous yellow and black golf umbrella
as he hurried to the rescue of the bride and her father.

'Oh, look, Jenni!' Rona said. 'It's the divine Carl!'

Jenni suppressed her irritation. It was indeed the
divine Carl. Trust him to turn up at exactly the right
moment and make an entrance! One of the things she'd
discovered about the new senior registrar since she'd
first met him on the ward, a week ago, was that he
liked to be centre stage.

As she watched him walking up the church path,
holding the umbrella over Trish and her father, Jenni
realised that she'd just thought of her new senior registrar as the divine Carl and that was something she'd
vowed she wouldn't do! It was the nickname that some
of the female staff had given to him when he'd first
arrived.

His name was Carl Devine, pronounced Deveen, but
so many of her nurses insisted on deliberately mispro-
nouncing his name that Jenni had already, albeit
unwillingly, followed suit!

As far as Jenni could see there was nothing remotely

divine about this man, even if he made it patently obvious that he thought there was! Unless, of course, she thought, you were one of those people who thought that good looks made a man godlike. Fortunately, she wasn't of that persuasion!

She retreated with the other guests into the church to make room for the bridal party, who were advancing up the path towards the porch. Steam was rising from the umbrellas set to dry beside the walls of the church. Damp hats had been removed to reveal squashed hairdos. Somewhere along the way she'd become separated from Rona in the crush.

'There's room for you here, Jenni.'

Jenni smiled, gratefully, as she squeezed in beside Hannah and Simon Delaware and their two small children in a pew at the back of the church.

'Thanks, Hannah. Oh, doesn't little Gwen look gorgeous? How old is she now?'

Dr Hannah Delaware cuddled her sleeping daughter. 'Ten months. She fell asleep in the car and I'm hoping she'll stay that way till the end of the service. There's absolutely no peace when she's awake.'

'Oh, she's beautiful. I remember the day she was born,' Jenni said fondly.

Simon Delaware leaned across his wife to speak to Jenni. 'Don't we all! That was the most eventful christening I've ever been to. Poor Lindy and Greg were trying to organise a civilised reception party for baby Thomas Charles, and Hannah disappeared upstairs to deliver herself of this little mini-tornado.'

Hannah grinned. 'There's gratitude for you! A house full of obstetricians and the only help I got was when Simon cut the cord, and that was only because I didn't have any scissors with me.'

'Exactly the same as when Jamie was born,' Simon said. 'Hannah delivered herself and then Bradley Prestcot arrived to cut the cord. I didn't get there until Jamie was nearly half an hour old.'

There was no disguising his admiration as he turned to look at his two-and-a-half-year-old son, who was studiously working his way through the hymn book.

The little boy was frowning. 'No pictures, Daddy.'

'Here, try this one,' Jenni said, pulling a small package from her large, overstuffed, leather shoulder-bag. 'Go on, Jamie, take the paper off.'

The little boy smiled happily as he extricated a small colouring-book and a packet of crayons.

Hannah's eyes widened in surprise. 'However did you come to have that with you, Jenni?'

Jenni smiled. 'I'm calling in to see my parents on the way back to hospital and their house is always overflowing with grandchildren at the weekend. It's OK, I've got more where that came from.'

'You're so good with children,' Hannah said. 'I've sometimes watched you on the ward and. . .'

'Oh, Hannah, I'm only doing my job.'

'It's more than that—you're a natural mother. You know, I really had to work at bonding with. . .'

'Hush, Hannah,' Simon said with mock severity. 'The bride's coming in.'

Hannah raised her eyebrows at Jenni and mouthed the word, 'Men!'

Jenni suppressed a giggle but at the same time she couldn't help wondering, as she always did when witnessing a dutiful wife being bossed around by a domineering husband, how on earth—or, indeed, why on earth—they put up with such impolite behaviour!

The organist had struck up the evocative opening

chords of the wedding march. Jenni strained her neck to see round the people standing at the entrance to the porch, shaking out their umbrellas.

Not the kind of weather Jenni had expected on Easter Saturday. But as she saw the radiant smile on the bride's face she realised that nothing could dampen Trish's spirits today. She was marrying Adam—the man of her dreams, as the romantic stories would call him. But once that ring was on her finger the poor girl would be on the slippery slope towards dutiful little wifey-hood!

'Is there room for a little one, Sister Dugdale?'

Jenni looked up as she heard the quietly spoken, smooth-voiced enquiry. 'Well, Dr Devine, we're already squashed but. . .'

'I can put Jamie on my lap,' Simon Delaware said, lifting his son who was still clutching the precious book and crayons in his tiny hands. Two of the crayons rolled on the floor and Jamie wriggled off Simon's lap to crawl under the pew.

Jenni suppressed a sigh of resignation. Having only spoken to Carl Devine whilst on duty, she would now have to make the effort to be socially polite. He was the sort of man who tended to bring out the worst in her because she longed to pull him down a peg or two! On the ward this week she'd been able to be utterly professional but here, in the closest proximity imaginable, it was going to be a strain.

As she stared ahead, watching the proceedings, she couldn't help but be aware of the slim, muscular thigh, encased in expensive, dark grey worsted, that was uncomfortably close to her skirt. She tried to inch herself the other way but came up against Hannah, cradling the sleeping Gwen.

'Sorry, Jenni, I can't move any further,' Hannah whispered.

Carl Devine leaned across in front of Jenni. 'No problem, Dr Delaware. There's plenty of room.'

Jenni caught a whiff of cologne and held her breath until Carl Devine had stopped speaking to Hannah. Being an obvious lady's man, he would go in for that sort of thing, she thought as she allowed the cologne to waft over her. Reluctantly, she had to admit that it wasn't altogether unpleasant.

Two small bridesmaids were holding the bride's ivory silk train, followed by two boys looking very self-conscious in black suits with white shirts.

The boys turned as they passed and Jenni recognised ten-year-old Michael Delaware and Edward, Trish's eight-year-old son.

'Hi, Mum,' Michael whispered to Hannah, a cheeky grin on his face.

'You look so smart!' Hannah whispered back.

Michael grimaced as he walked on and Hannah, risking Simon's wrath, leaned towards Jenni and whispered, 'Trish had a hard time talking Michael into this. She wanted Edward to be a page boy but he said he wouldn't do it unless Michael was with him.'

Jenni watched the bridal party move slowly down the aisle until she could see that Trish had arrived at the front of the church, and was now standing next to Adam.

The vicar was exhorting everyone to stand for the first hymn. Jenni was glad she'd worn her higher-than-average heels on her long legs. Carl Devine was very tall, but she didn't feel overpowered by his height. Glancing sideways, she could see that she was almost up to his ear. His hair was distinctly casual in appearance, quite long in fact. And he needed a shave—or was the designer stubble for effect?

His hair was almost black, with a hint of gold, she noticed. She'd once had a favourite cat with fur that was almost the same colour. For a split second she felt the desire to raise her hand and touch it to see if it felt the same as Brindle's.

She coloured as he turned to see her studying him. He smiled as he opened his hymn book and began to sing in a deeply resonant voice. Good thing he didn't know she'd been comparing him with her cat!

It was a beautiful service. Two young nurses in the pew in front sniffed as they stifled their tears at the end, and Jenni passed them some tissues from her bag. Trish and Adam walked past, looking blissfully happy as they proceeded into the porch.

'Are you going to the reception, Sister?' Carl Devine asked.

'Isn't everyone?'

'I was wondering if you could show me the way over to Bramdale? I'll follow your car.'

'Actually, I left my car at the hospital and came with Staff Nurse Phillips.'

'Oh, good; even better, you can ride with me.'

Jenni tensed. It would have been better if he'd asked if she wanted to ride with him. But the thought of another ten miles of Rona's chatter was decidedly unappealing!

She found Rona and explained that Dr Devine had asked her to show him the way to the reception. Rona's eyes appeared to stand out on stalks! Jenni, anxious to avoid the expected innuendoes, hurried along to speak to the bride and groom.

'Congratulations! You look lovely, Trish.'

'Thank goodness it's stopped raining,' Adam said. 'We were thinking of holding the wedding in the car and asking all of you to come out of the church and stand around in the rain.'

'Then Carl Devine came to the rescue,' Trish said. 'I hope he knows he's invited to the reception. I haven't had time since he arrived this week to send him a formal invitation.'

'He knows,' Jenni said. 'I'm going to show him the way over to Bramdale.'

Trish smiled. 'How kind. Come on, Jenni, join in this group photograph. Everybody smile at the camera. Cheese!'

The photographer was still snapping when Carl Devine put his hand under Jenni's arm and tried to steer her away.

'Why don't we escape before the traffic jam? This part of the wedding always bores me. Standing around in graveyards isn't my scene.'

Jenni smiled. 'Nor mine.' Good to find they had something in common!

He opened the passenger door and she curled her long legs underneath her.

'Weddings are OK for the half-hour service but the bits that follow are so tedious, Sister,' Carl Devine said, as he roared off down the road, away from the church.

'Oh, I agree,' Jenni said. 'Probably preparing the happy couple for the tedious years that lie ahead, don't you think, Dr Devine?'

Carl Devine laughed. 'My sentiments exactly. Can't see the point of getting hitched for a lifetime of domestic bliss. Look, shall we skip the formal title? Call me Carl.'

'And I'm Jenni.'

'I know, but I thought I'd better not jump the gun and risk getting my head snapped off.'

They were passing over the humpback bridge in the middle of the village and Jenni clung to the seat. 'How do you mean, get your head snapped off?'

'Well, you haven't exactly welcomed me on to the ward with open arms.'

'Dr Devine. . .I mean Carl, the smooth running of my ward is the only thing that matters when I'm on duty. I've no time for people who want to indulge in social chit-chat in working hours.'

'Oops, sorry, Sister! So what are you like off duty, Jenni?'

He glanced sideways and Jenni felt a rush of colour to her face. His dark eyes were very probing.

'Well, I'm off duty now so you can judge for yourself.'

'Still waters run deep,' he murmured, half to himself as he kept his eyes studiously on the road. 'I think that under that austere veneer of professional perfection beats the heart of a warm, fun-loving young girl.'

'Less of the young. I've just turned thirty.'

'Positively one foot in the grave. I'm six years older than you so I think you should give me some respect for my grey hairs.'

She laughed. 'What grey hairs?'

They were driving over the brow of the hill that led away from Cragdale over the moors to the more remote dales. Carl pulled the car onto a strip of moorland at the side of the road.

'Let me show you,' he said with an amused grin as he switched off the engine and ran his fingers through his hair. 'Just behind my ears, here, there's a whole crop.'

Jenni leaned forward to get a better look. 'Good heavens! You're right. There must be at least half a dozen lurking there. Shall I pull them out for you?'

'No, I've decided to keep them. They're my battle scars. Evidence that I've lived life to the full.'

She moved back against her own seat. The solemn expression in his brown eyes was totally at odds with the devil-may-care character traits she'd attributed to him. She was intrigued.

'Care to tell me about it?' she asked lightly.

The enigmatic expression vanished and his eyes glinted mischievously. 'We'd be here all night and that wouldn't do your image any good, Sister.'

'Ah, so you think I have an image to live up to, do you?'

'In hospital, most definitely. That's why I wanted to spend some time getting to know you today while we're both off duty. It will make life so much easier when we're working together. When you give me the cold shoulder on the ward I won't take it personally.'

'If I give you the cold shoulder, as you put it, it's usually because I'm rushed off my feet and haven't time for anything but my patients.'

He smiled. 'Oh, I have noticed that you put your babies before your staff.'

She liked the way he smiled—good firm teeth—it made him look much younger. She'd never imagined that he'd been analysing her behaviour all week.

She smiled back. 'And why shouldn't I put the babies first? They can't speak up for themselves. They need somebody to champion their demands.'

'And what a champion they have in Sister Jenni Dugdale. It's lucky for them that you're so single-minded.'

'I'm only doing my job, as I constantly remind people,' she said quickly. 'Don't you think we should be moving along? Any minute now the bridal party will. . .'

'Here they come!' Carl said, as the white Rolls Royce cleared the brow of the hill.

He restarted the engine. Jenni smiled stoically as her colleagues in the passing cars gave them curious glances.

'So much for beating the traffic jam,' she said as they joined the back of the wedding procession. 'We should have kept moving.'

But as they drove slowly over the moorland road, following the string of cars, she couldn't help thinking that she was glad they'd stopped for those few minutes. She was beginning to think that Carl Devine wasn't the shallow extrovert she'd taken him for.

There was more to him than met the eye. In the week since he'd first arrived on her ward she'd been fooled by his carefree manner, but that sensitive look in his eyes just now had given him away. It was as if he'd been sounding her out, wondering if he could trust her enough to reveal his true personality.

They followed the wedding procession across the moorland road between the two valleys and drove down into Bramdale. It was a quieter valley than Cragdale with fewer houses. Jenni pointed out the house where the reception was to be held.

'As you can see, it's a very large old house. It's been converted into an infertility clinic. Adam is the director and Trish is one of the specialist doctors. Trish and Adam met while they were working at Moortown General last year. We all thought they would eventually get together but it wasn't an easy romance.'

'What romance ever is?' Carl said wryly, as he steered the car into the large grounds.

'Do I take it you're speaking from your vast experience?'

'Oh, absolutely! Tell me, Jenni, do Trish and Adam live in the Bramdale clinic?'

Jenni nodded. 'In that new wing over there. That's where the reception is.'

As she climbed out of the car she looked up at the tall oak trees in the extensive grounds that reached down to the river.

'Impressive, isn't it?' she said.

Carl nodded. 'It's an idyllic setting. I wouldn't mind a transfer from Moortown General. For a start, there's this ogre of a sister on the ward where I work.'

'Must be terrible for you,' Jenni said.

She became separated from Carl as they made their way through the crowd of guests to the large drawing-room, where canapés and champagne were being served. This was followed by a buffet of cold meats, salads, creamy desserts and fruit.

Jenni was pressed into joining a group of her nurses at a table near the bay window overlooking the lawn. Outside, the sun was shining down on the grass and a warm haze rose up towards the lilac and laburnum trees where she thought she could discern a hint of early blue and yellow blossoms.

She listened to the chatter and joined in occasionally, whilst wishing that she could wander down to the river and escape the interminable hospital gossip.

Every time she looked across the room she could see Carl Devine, surrounded by a sycophantic crowd. Loud shrieks of laughter came from his female admirers. It would be difficult for him not to become big-headed!

Well, so long as he was skilful and efficient in his work she wouldn't mind.

She glanced at her watch. She and Rona would have to leave soon. They were both on duty this evening.

A passing waitress poured her another cup of tea. She'd declined the champagne because she didn't like drinking before she went on duty.

'What a beautiful house!'

She looked up at the sound of Carl's voice.

'Yes, it's lovely.'

'I came to see if you'd like a lift back to hospital at the end of the reception.'

She hesitated. 'I think Rona's expecting me to go with her. Actually, I've got to make a slight detour to call in on my parents for a few minutes, so. . .'

'No problem.' He smiled. 'I'll disentangle you from Rona.' He moved away before she could protest.

As she watched him speaking to Rona she frowned. Why was she letting him take charge of her arrangements? Was it the fact that he'd accused her of being less than welcoming with him when he'd first arrived? Was she trying to overcompensate for her lack of warmth? Or was she intrigued by his personality, and hoping to find out more about him?

Reluctantly, she admitted to herself that the latter was nearer the truth.

She could see Rona smiling and nodding at Carl in an obsequiously over-enchanted way. It was pathetic, the way some women overreacted when they chatted to an attractive man! But what was it that made him so attractive to the opposite sex? Was it the way he smiled? She herself had admired that one! Was it the tall, slim, athletic build?

His huge shoulders tapered down to a narrow waist,

she noticed. The cut of his dark grey suit was impeccable. As he finished speaking she saw his lips move to a slightly pursed position—a deliberately determined jutting forward of the chin that made him look like a man of action.

Oh, God! He'd caught her studying him again! He was coming over. She took a deep breath, before occupying herself by saying goodbye to all her friends. She wasn't going to have him think that she was falling under his spell like the rest of the female staff. That would be the day!

They slipped away as unobtrusively as possible after saying goodbye to Trish and Adam.

'So, where do your parents live?' Carl asked as he steered the car carefully down the gravel drive past the long line of parked cars.

'In Riversdale. It's a few miles off the Moortown road.' She gave him the necessary directions. 'I'm surprised you didn't want to stay longer at the reception.'

'I promised Simon Delaware to hold the fort this evening.'

'Always a good idea to keep in with your consultant.'

'Exactly! And it also gives me the chance to make a good impression on the Nightingale sister so she'll be kind to me on the ward—maybe even make me the odd cup of coffee.'

Jenni laughed. 'I wouldn't have thought you needed to beg for a cup of coffee. My nursing staff seem to fall over themselves to grant your every whim.'

He gave an over-exaggerated sigh. 'I know. But coffee served from your own fair hands, Sister, would. . .'

'There's our farmhouse!' she interrupted, glad of an excuse to cut short his stage performance. Why did he have to revert to the charming façade? She much preferred the warm character she glimpsed when he was off guard.

'How old is it?' he asked as he drove down the steep hillside road.

'The original part was built in the thirteenth century and it's been added to over the years. Our ancestors used to farm all the land in the valley. Little by little they sold off the land, and when my father decided not to go into farming my grandmother sold off the remaining fields. That was when the property developers had given her an offer she couldn't refuse.'

She pointed through the open window. 'That cluster of so-called desirable residences down there beside the river is built on the land Grandma sold.'

'Well, at least they're in keeping with the landscape.'

'That was one thing Grandma insisted upon before she sold the land. But it was a good move from a financial point of view. She shared the money among her grandchildren, which meant that we've all been able to buy our own houses.'

'Yes, I heard you'd got a place in Cragdale.'

'Been checking up on me, have you, Doctor?'

'Not difficult in a hospital with the most efficient grapevine in medical history.'

Jenni showed Carl where to turn the car off the main road.

'What an interesting-looking house!' he said as he drove through the wooden gates and down the ancient, cobblestoned track.

'Yes, I love this place. I'm always glad I was actually born here,' Jenni said, climbing out of the car.

'We all were. Mum moved in here when she married Dad, and the children arrived in quick succession. First

Mum had twins—my brother Gavin and my sister Gemma—then Freddy came along the following year and a couple of years later I put in my appearance.'

He smiled. 'So you're the baby of the family.'

'And the only unmarried one. The others have all got families of their own now. Eleven children between them, can you believe? Gemma has three daughters, Gavin three boys and a girl, and Freddy two of each.'

She looked up at the dark grey, uneven stones and felt the familiar rush of happiness at being home. It was like a pilgrimage that she had to make every weekend, if only for a few minutes when her duties would allow.

There was a shriek of delight as two small fair-haired girls rushed out of the house.

'Jenni! Jenni!'

Tiny hands were reaching up to be lifted into Jenni's arms.

'These are my brother Freddy's children. Felicity is five and Naomi is four. This is Carl, girls.'

The little girls gave a shy smile at the stranger, but kept their little arms tightly around their aunt's neck.

Jenni led the way along the uneven, flagstoned passage that led to the huge, high-ceilinged kitchen, where she knew she would find her mother. Mrs Dugdale smiled with pleasure as she looked up from the cake she was dusting with icing sugar.

'Hello, what a lovely surprise!' She was smiling directly at Carl. 'I'm Susan.'

Carl smiled back at the tall, pretty, fair-haired lady and held out his hand. 'I'm Carl.'

'My hands are too sugary to shake, Carl,' Mrs Dugdale said with a light, tinkling laugh. 'I've got to finish this cake for tea. Jenni, put the kettle on.'

'We can't stay, Mum,' Jenni said as she filled the

kettle, and placed it on the hob at the edge of the huge black kitchen range where a fire smouldered gently.

Having done this, she produced books and pencils for Felicity and Naomi and settled them on chairs at the kitchen table.

'I'm on duty at six. I just popped in with these colouring-books for the girls. Where's Dad?'

'Gone to one of his meetings. He'll be so disappointed to miss you. Can't you possibly stay on for supper?'

Jenni shook her head. 'Sorry, Mum. The staffing rota is in chaos because of Trish's and Adam's wedding so I put myself down for tonight.'

'When I was a staff nurse I used to make sure I got my Saturday nights free,' Mrs Dugdale said, looking across at Carl as if seeking moral support.

'I can't think where my daughter gets all this devotion to duty from.'

'Who else is here?' Jenni said quickly.

'No one. I've got Felicity and Naomi all to myself. I'm looking after them for the weekend while Freddy and Megan are in Paris for that medical conference. They've left Charles and baby Stephen with Megan's mum.'

'Freddy's a surgeon in Leeds,' Jenni explained as she leaned over to admire the artistic masterpieces her nieces were producing at the kitchen table.

'Megan used to be a staff nurse,' Mrs Dugdale said, moving her cake out of the way of the enthusiastic artists. 'But, of course, she gave up working when she had the children.'

'Of course,' Jenni said wryly. 'Megan is the perfect little wife.'

'Now don't start all that again,' her mother said.

Jenni knew that the smile on her mother's face was designed to soften her peremptory tone, but she could tell that she was annoyed.

'Jenni seems to think that babies can bring themselves up while their mothers continue with their careers, Carl.'

Jenni smiled. 'It's all a matter of choice. If Megan had chosen to stay on at the hospital she would have been a sister by now.'

'And what about her beautiful family?'

'Mum, this is the twentieth century. Freddy and Megan could easily afford a live-in nanny.'

She glanced up at Carl, who was leaning against the wall—an amused smile on his face.

'I'm sorry. I'll come down off my soap-box.'

Susan Dugdale laughed. 'Jenni easily gets carried away with her strange ideas. I was more than happy to give up my nursing career to take care of my four children. And as for putting up with a live-in nanny. . .! Your father would never have allowed that.'

Jenni hurriedly changed the topic of conversation by launching into a description of Trish's and Adam's wedding, after which her mother insisted they try a piece of her sponge cake and drink a cup of tea.

Jenni finished her cake, glanced at the grandfather clock and said that they really would have to go back to hospital. Mrs Dugdale saw them off at the kitchen door, her grandchildren waving their colouring-books.

'Daddy will be so sorry to have missed you. Come again soon, won't you?'

'Dad used to be headmaster at Moortown High,' Jenni explained as they drove off.

'He retired last year but still gets asked to attend various meetings. I used to find it so embarassing, having my father as head of my school. But, apart from that, I had a really happy childhood. I still get on really well with my brothers, Freddy and Gavin, and my sister, Gemma, even though they're all married and living away from home.'

'You're lucky to have such a close-knit family. I'm surprised you haven't got married yourself and started your own family by now.'

'You must be joking! Give up my freedom to some domineering man? Not in a million years. I've seen my mother fetching my father's slippers like a pet poodle. I've watched my brothers being dictatorial to their wives over something really simple like where they should go for their holidays. And the men always got their way! Can you believe it?'

Carl laughed. 'Yes, I can believe it. But don't you feel you're missing out by not having a family of your own?'

'Oh, I'd love a baby!'

As soon as she'd made the confession she wished she'd kept her mouth shut. She'd never told anyone how she longed for a baby of her own.

Since hitting thirty a couple of months ago, she'd become obsessed with the idea. She adored looking after the babies on her ward. But it wasn't the same as having a baby of her own and she realised that the biological clock was ticking away.

'Well, you can't have your cake and eat it,' Carl said. 'You can't be a mum and retain your uncommitted freedom.'

'It's not totally out of the question,' she said quietly.

He shot her a startled glance. 'What do you mean?'

She hesitated. 'I don't think it would pose any problems that couldn't be surmounted. . . But I've said too much already. I'd rather you didn't repeat my words to anybody.'

'Oh, for heaven's sake, Jenni! I know you were only joking. I realise that. . . Jenni? You were joking, weren't you?'

They were driving down into Moortown. The Saturday night crowds were gathering outside the cinema. This was the strangest conversation to be having with a man who would soon be walking down the ward and speaking to her about their professional duties.

'Please, Carl. Forget what I've just told you. I don't know why I've confided in you like this. I hardly know you and. . .'

He took one hand from the wheel and covered hers.

'Don't worry, Jenni, I've forgotten everything you said. But if ever you want to bring up the subject again feel free. Maybe I could help you. I mean, it always helps to discuss a problem, doesn't it?'

CHAPTER TWO

IT WAS a week since Carl had driven Jenni back to hospital from the wedding reception. As she sat at the desk in her office behind the nurses' station she found herself wondering, for the umpteenth time, why on earth she'd confided her deepest wish to a man she hardly knew. It certainly hadn't made it any easier for her to work with him here on the Nightingale wing.

She put down her pen from the report she was trying to write and leaned back in her chair. She'd caught him watching her closely on several occasions as they'd worked together during the past week. Was she being over-sensitive? After all, he hadn't tried to make conversation with her. They'd simply been doing their jobs together.

Talking of which, she really ought to get out there on the ward! She would finish the report later. She had a good team of nurses but she needed to keep her finger on the pulse.

She rolled down the sleeves of her royal blue uniform dress and slipped on the white starched cuffs. Glancing in the mirror, she repinned her frilly sister's cap. It was important to look neat and tidy on the ward. A wisp of the long blonde hair she'd pinned underneath fell down over her forehead. She searched for a hair grip in her desk drawer, returned to the mirror and secured the straying strands in place.

Someone was knocking, and in the mirror she could see the door opening.

'Don't hide all your hair away, Jenni. It makes you look too severe.'

She turned and faced Carl Devine. 'Yes, but it's practical. It's unhygienic to have hair falling all over my patients.'

He grinned. 'You're not going to ask me to have my hair cut, are you, Sister?'

She moved towards him. 'I might suggest it if it gets much longer.'

She looked up at his distinctively coloured hair. 'There's a hint of gold there, isn't there? Most unusual.'

'Dad's hair was black, Mum's hair was gold.'

She was enjoying herself! 'Ah, that accounts for it. I actually wondered if you were related to one of the cats we had when I was a child. It had flecks of gold amongst the black.'

He pulled a wry face. 'You certainly know how to keep a chap in his place.'

She smiled. 'That was meant to be a compliment. Brindle had lovely fur. He won a prize at the Riversdale show.'

'Oh, well, in that case I'm truly flattered!'

'Actually, he was the only one entered in the brindle class,' she added, trying hard to keep a straight face.

He laughed. 'Once more I'm utterly deflated. I don't know whether I dare tell you the reason I came to see you.'

'Try me,' she said lightly, wondering why on earth she was being so facetious in the middle of a morning on the ward. It was so unprofessional. Carl Devine was having an adverse effect on her. If she'd caught one of her nurses chatting away like this she'd have given her a mild ticking-off!

'I popped in to see if you'll come out for a drink

with me tonight. I'd like to check out this excellent pub that everybody keeps talking about—the Coach and Horses. So I need a native guide.'

She opened her blue eyes wide in mock astonishment. 'You mean you've been here two weeks and haven't been to the Coach and Horses? I would have thought some of my nurses would have dragged you up there by now.'

'Oh, they tried, but I was saving myself for the Nightingale boss. So, are you free, Jenni?'

'I've got a really busy schedule today.'

'That's no answer. What are you doing tonight?'

She hesitated. 'I could maybe drive out there by about eight.'

What was she saying? There were masses of things to be done at the cottage. She'd planned a quiet night in to catch up with the ironing and. . .

'I'll pick you up from your house in Cragdale at about seven forty-five.'

'Hold on a minute. Maybe it would be better if. . .'

The door opened and Staff Nurse Carol Thomas walked in. 'Sorry to interrupt, Sister, but Mrs Fowlds is asking for you in the gynae unit. She's getting herself worked up again.'

'I'll come now.'

Jenni was halfway out of the door, with Carl following close behind.

'That's the patient who's asking for a hysterectomy, isn't it?' Carl said as they moved swiftly along the corridor towards the gynaecology unit. 'Fill me in on the details.'

Jenni nodded. 'Sally Fowlds is thirty-one; she's having excessive, prolonged menstruation and she persuaded her GP to have her admitted for a hysterectomy.

But Simon Delaware is holding off for the time being. He's not convinced it's necessary.'

'Neither am I,' Carl said. 'I remember discussing the case with Simon, and we both came to the same conclusion.'

Jenni glanced up at him. 'Then do I take it you're an advocate of conservative treatment?'

'In some cases, yes. Mrs Fowlds has been checked for fibroids and endometriosis, hasn't she?'

'Yes. The results were negative.'

They had reached the gynae unit. Their plump, fair-haired patient was sitting in a chair beside her bed, sobbing quietly, while a young junior nurse stood beside her, holding her hand.

Jenni told the nurse that she would take over.

'Now, Sally, tell me what's the matter,' she said gently as she pulled up a stool and sat down beside her patient.

'It should have all been over by now but nobody's taking any notice of me,' Sally Fowlds sobbed.

'Now that's where you're wrong, Sally,' Carl said in a soothing voice as he leaned against the side of the bed. 'Mr Delaware and I have given a lot of thought to your case and we've decided that you'll be better off without a hysterectomy because. . .'

'But I've got these awful periods, Doctor. Sometimes I only get a couple of weeks off in the middle of the month and then I'm on again.'

Carl leaned forward and took hold of the patient's hand.

'Sally, we know that. But there are other ways of dealing with heavy bleeding, besides taking out your womb. Now, we've tested you for fibroids—you're clear; we've checked for endometriosis, that is to say any abnormalities of the womb lining. And. . .'

He turned to look at Jenni. 'What was the result of the biopsy we took, Sister?'

Jenni handed over the notes, which she'd already scanned. 'Absolutely no malignancy, Dr Devine.'

Sally Fowlds had become very quiet. 'So what are you going to do about my heavy periods, Doctor? If I didn't have a womb I wouldn't have anything to trouble me so. . .'

'Sally, you're only thirty-one. If you were suffering from endometriosis or malignancy or huge fibroids then we would have to resort to surgery, but in your case an operation may not be the answer. There can sometimes be side-effects from removing the womb, you know.'

The patient wiped a hand over her face and Jenni handed her a tissue.

'What kind of side-effects?' Sally Fowlds asked in a small voice.

'Come with me,' Carl said, putting out his hands to help the patient stand up.

Mrs Fowlds knotted the belt around her white towelling dressing-gown. 'Where are we going?'

'I'm going to introduce you to another patient in a nearby cubicle.'

Jenni followed patient and doctor into Jean Crabtree's cubicle, thinking that Carl certainly had some novel ways of dealing with his patients!

Jean Crabtree, a small, dark-haired woman, was leaning back against her pillows. She gave a wan smile when she saw Carl.

'Hello, Jean. How are you, today?'

'I'm feeling a bit weak, Doctor.'

Carl took hold of the patient's hand and gave her an encouraging smile.

'That's only to be expected at the moment, Jean. That's why we admitted you. But you should start to feel better soon. I've brought you a visitor. This is Sally Fowlds. She's wondering whether to have a hysterectomy to get rid of her heavy periods. That's what you did five years ago isn't it, Jean?'

'Did it cure you?' Sally asked eagerly.

Jean pulled a wry face. 'Oh, my periods stopped. But I was only twenty-eight and I went into an early menopause.'

'Even though the surgeon had left Jean's ovaries intact it still didn't stop the hot flushes, severe sweating and aching joints,' Jenni added, realising what Carl was trying to achieve.

'Of course, not everybody suffers like Jean during the menopause. Some people sail through with few problems, but in Jean's case she had to put up with an awful lot of discomfort.'

'I'm only thirty-three now,' Jean said wearily, 'and the last five years have been most unpleasant, to put it mildly.'

'The most serious side-effect was the onset of osteoporosis,' Carl said quietly.

He was watching Sally intently to judge her reaction.

'A condition where you have thinning, brittle bones when you're only twenty-eight isn't much fun. Now, I'm not saying this always happens. A large percentage of hysterectomies are completely successful, but in certain cases the operation can have unpleasant side-effects. So I think we should be aware of the dangers.'

Carl and Jenni took Sally back to her own cubicle, telling Jean that they would return shortly.

'So how will you cure me, Doctor?' Sally asked.

'I'm proposing to fit you with a hormone-releasing intra-uterine device.'

He smiled at his patient. 'Don't be alarmed at the highfaluting name. All it means is that you will have a small device placed inside your womb that will slowly release small ammounts of levonorgestrel, the hormone used in some contraceptive pills. We've discovered that this can reduce menstrual bleeding by up to ninety per cent.'

'It's worth a try,' Jenni said encouragingly.

'Is that what you'd do, Sister, if you were me?'

'Most definitely. You've had all the children you want so now. . .'

'Have you got kids, Sister?'

The question took Jenni by surprise.

'Not yet,' she replied quietly.

Carl was looking at her with an enigmatic expression. She coloured as she looked away. Why had she said that? Why hadn't she simply said that she didn't have any children?

'Now just rest, Sally,' Carl said quickly. 'Let me know what you decide.'

They went back to Jean Crabtree's cubicle.

'Thanks, Jean,' Carl said. 'You were a great help.'

The patient smiled. 'How soon before my own treatment will take effect, Doctor?'

'You're having a large doseage of hormones so you should be feeling better in a few days. Have the aches in your joints eased, Jean?'

'Not really.'

'I think physiotherapy would help,' Jenni said. 'Some gentle exercises would stop the joints from stiffening.'

'I agree,' Carl said. 'Would you arrange that, Sister?'

Jenni nodded. 'Of course. And while you're waiting for the physiotherapist to arrive you could take a little walk down to the day-room, Jean. It's much more interesting down there than lying here in bed.'

Jenni called over one of the nurses to help Jean out of bed, before going over to the phone and ringing the physiotherapy department.

'Don't go,' she said to Carl. 'I want you to see a patient in the postnatal unit. I think we're going to have to put her on antibiotics.'

Carl waited until she'd instructed the physiotherapy department about Jean Crabtree.

'I think you could run Nightingale on your own, Jenni,' he said wryly, as they walked along the corridor to the obstetrics unit. 'You don't really need a doctor.'

Jenni smiled. 'I need you to rubber-stamp my ideas. And, occasionally, you come up with some good ideas of your own—like taking Sally Fowlds to see Jean Crabtree. I wasn't sure what you were up to at first.'

He grinned. 'I'm glad you approve. I was quaking in my shoes, expecting you to slap me on the wrist, Sister. But I must admit you've mellowed since I first arrived a couple of weeks ago.'

'You really do exaggerate, Carl,' Jenni said lightly. But she knew he was right. Since getting to know him better on Trish's and Adam's wedding day she'd changed her attitude towards him.

He pushed open the door to the postnatal unit and Jenni felt a rush of pleasure as she heard the sounds of the newborn babies. She loved walking in here. She knew every single baby by name and she could remember their birth weights without checking on the chart. It was as if each one was her very own child.

Bending over the first cot, she picked up the tiny, crying baby and cradled him in her arms.

'Jonathan, my little lamb, what a noise! Are you hungry, my pet?'

Little red-faced Jonathan stopped crying and opened his mouth to snuffle along Jenni's apron.

'I haven't got anything for you there, Jonathan,' Jenni said. 'Let's see if we can persuade Mummy to feed you.'

She looked at the empty bed beside the cot. 'Where's Madelaine?'

Small, blonde Staff Nurse Penny Drew looked uncomfortable.

'Madelaine's gone to the day-room for a smoke, Sister.'

Jenni frowned. 'Would you like to tell Madelaine that baby Jonathan is ready for his feed, Staff Nurse?'

The baby, becoming impatient again, had started to wail. Jenni lifted him gently over her shoulder, soothing him with her hands until he was quiet. Looking up, she realised that Carl was still with her—watching every move she made.

'About the patient I'm supposed to see,' he said quietly.

'Oh, yes, I'll be along in a minute. She's in cubicle six. Julie Branton. She appears to be developing mastitis so I think she needs antibiotics.'

'I'm sure your diagnosis will be correct, Sister,' Carl said wryly. He lowered his voice. 'I hope you're not going to tear a strip off Jonathan's poor little mum for smoking.'

Jenni pursed her lips. 'No, but I'll get the message across.'

'I'm sure you will,' Carl said as he moved along to check on their mastitis patient.

'Ah, there you are, Madelaine,' Jenni said as the baby's mother walked back into her cubicle. 'Jonathan's been telling me he's hungry.'

'He's always hungry.' Madelaine Farrow ran a hand through her long auburn hair. 'Why can't one of the nurses give him a bottle when he cries?'

Jenni was trying hard not to let her distaste for the smell of smoky breath that was drifting across the cubicle interfere with her concern for mother and baby—especially for baby!

'Yes, it would be possible for one of the nurses to give Jonathan a bottle,' Jennie said carefully. 'But your milk is better for him and I remember you telling me, soon after he was born, that you wanted to feed him yourself.'

'Well, that was before I knew what hard work it was. I thought it would be easier than cleaning out all those bottles and mixing up feeds and all that. But here in hospital the nurses could do all that for me for a few days, couldn't they?'

'Madelaine, breast-feeding isn't something you can leave for a few days if you don't feel like it,' Jenni explained as patiently as she could. 'If the milk supply isn't stimulated by sucking or expressing every few hours it simply dries up.'

'Oh, all right,' Madelaine said sulkily as she climbed onto her bed. 'Pass him over here, Sister.'

Jenni took a deep breath to stop herself from snapping. Carefully she placed the baby in his mother's arms.

How could any woman be so indifferent to such a wonderful child? But, then, Madeleine was only seventeen. Maybe she would feel differently about babies when she reached the ripe old age of thirty and realised how precious they were!

Jenni waited until baby Jonathan had latched onto his mother's nipple and begun to suck voraciously.

'He's so greedy, Sister,' Madelaine said. 'I fed him just before I had breakfast and now just look at him!'

'Madelaine, that was nearly four hours ago.'

Jenni picked up the feeds chart. Nothing had been entered today. She made a mental note to ask all the nursing staff to check up on this.

'You know, Sister, I don't think I'm cut out to be a mother,' Madelaine said quietly. 'My boyfriend, Nick, wanted this baby, but I didn't. He said it would bring us closer together. Hah! He hasn't been in for two days.'

Jenni made another mental note to check with the social services. In Madelaine's case notes she'd read that the young couple had been living with Madelaine's grandmother. Madelaine and baby Jonathan could have gone home already under normal circumstances, but there was now a problem about where they were going to live.

Grandma had apparently decided that she didn't want them back.

'I'll come and see you again later, Madelaine,' Jenni said.

As she went out of the cubicle she realised that she hadn't discussed smoking with the young mother. It wasn't a good time to bring it up now. The poor girl had enough worries. And at least she'd gone down to the day-room for her smoke.

Madelaine hadn't forced her baby to breathe in the dangerous fumes. Not since he was born, anyway. But Jenni constantly worried about the fact that Jonathan had been a tiny underweight baby at birth, typical of so many infants of smoking mothers that she'd delivered.

And what would happen when Madelaine took the baby away from hospital? She wouldn't be so careful about not smoking near the baby then. Jenni knew that she would have to pick a good time to have a serious chat with Madelaine, for baby Jonathan's sake.

Going into cubicle six, she found Carl writing up antibiotics on Julie Branton's chart while one of the nurses was tidying the sheets and cover of the bed. She smiled at her patient.

'Sorry I took so long to get here, Julie.'

'I've examined Julie and she's got mastitis in the left breast,' Carl said, 'so I've asked her not to feed on that side.'

'You can feed with the right breast, Julie,' Jenni said, 'and you must express the milk from the left breast with your hand.'

'Yes, Dr Devine told me,' Julie said.

'And we've taken a specimen of milk to go to the lab for culture,' Carl said. 'Don't worry, Julie, the antibiotics will soon sort the problem out.'

Jenni walked back towards her office with Carl. She ought to get on with that report, but then again. . . She paused with her hand on the door.

'Would you like a quick coffee, Carl?'

He smiled. 'At last I've grovelled my way into the inner sanctum. Yes, please. I thought you'd never ask.'

Jenni saw that there was a half-full cafetière on the hot plate and deduced that Staff Nurse Carol Thomas must have taken her coffee-break. She poured out a couple of cups and settled herself in one of the armchairs. Carl found himself a chair nearby.

'Why is it that the good mothers get problems they don't deserve, Carl?' she said.

'Is that a rhetorical question or. . .?'

'I mean, take Julie Branton. She's an excellent mother and she's laid up with mastitis. Madelaine Farrow couldn't care less about baby Jonathan and she's in perfect health.'

'Julie's thirty-five, whereas Madelaine is only seventeen,' Carl said. 'It's not easy to be a parent at seventeen when you're little more than a child yourself.'

'You sound as if you're sympathetic towards Madelaine,' Jenni said. 'I know she's got problems but she tries my patience to the full.'

'She needs tender loving care, just like the baby,' Carl said quietly.

She looked up at him. 'But don't you think it's dreadful that Madelaine is so irresponsible towards her child?'

His eyes held a veiled expression. 'I'm a doctor. I simply try to solve the medical problems as they arise. I make a point of not being judgemental. Maybe Madelaine doesn't want this baby, but he's here now. She and her boyfriend will just have to get on with it. They'll make out, one way or another.'

Jenni put her cup down on the desk. Some of the coffee splattered out into the saucer. 'Yes, but what about baby Jonathan? He didn't ask to be born, but he's got saddled with two adolescent parents who. . .'

'Jenni, I don't think you know the first thing about what goes on in the real world.'

Carl stood up. 'Cocooned in your ideal family, you've never had to grow up. Thanks for the coffee.'

She stared at the closing door and, to her amazement, she found that she was close to tears. Carl's unexpected outburst had affected her profoundly. Had she really been cocooned in an ideal family? Was this longing for a baby to prove that she was an adult?

She picked up a tissue and dabbed her face. No, it was more than that. She took a deep breath. How dared Carl speak to her like that! Well, one thing was for sure, they wouldn't be going out together this evening. Of all the insufferable. . .

The door was opening. Carl was walking towards her.

'I'm sorry, Jenni. I shouldn't have said that.'

He was standing close to her chair, looking down at her with concern in his expressive eyes.

'You've got a nerve,' she said quietly, aware that her pulse was racing impossibly fast. His nearness was upsetting her. She could smell that distinctive cologne again.

'Are we still friends?'

She made a deliberately exaggerated sniff. 'I'll have to think about it.'

He gave her a wry grin. 'Will you have time to think before seven forty-five this evening?'

She could feel her good humour returning. The temporary depression was evaporating. 'I might, if you get yourself out of my office and give me a chance to do some work.'

He smiled broadly. 'Of course, oh queen.'

He was backing towards the door, his arm held across his chest in an approximation of a regal gesture.

As the door closed behind him she realised that the façade was back. For one brief instant he'd revealed his true character again—a man with profound opinions on a difficult subject. But why had he snapped her head off like that?

For the rest of the day she found herself racing against time to get everything finished before her evening off when she would hand over the reins to Staff Nurse Carol Thomas.

Promptly at six o'clock she gave Carol a brief report, before having a final check on the mother and baby unit to make sure there were no problems. By six-fifteen she was driving out of the car park and heading towards Cragdale.

As she drove down the steep hill towards her cottage she could see the sun sinking behind the moors, casting a broad band of orange light over the valley. Bluebells carpeted the woods and the lilac and laburnum in the gardens were in full bloom now. She realised that she was very lucky to live in such beautiful countryside.

As she manoeuvred the car up the narrow drive into her cottage garden she thought briefly about Madelaine and baby Jonathan and the difficult life ahead of them. Maybe Carl was right—she shouldn't be judgemental. She herself had so many advantages.

She looked up at the front of her cottage. The cream paint round the windows contrasted sharply with the dark, millstone grit. She was relieved to see that the ivy she was training to twine over the porch was definitely getting the message.

It was two years since she'd moved in, and there were still so many things that she wanted to do. The garden took up a lot of time in the summer, but it was worth it. It was all part of the dream she was working towards.

She smiled as she let herself in through the brass-studded oak door, lifting up the letters and junk mail from the mat with WELCOME inscribed upon it. This was her own little kingdom. All she needed now to make it really into a home was her very own baby—a baby who would be loved and cherished and welcomed by everybody in her family.

She went into the tiny kitchen at the back of the house and made herself a cup of tea. She drank it whilst she worked her way through the pile of ironing, carefully selecting her favourite cream silk blouse for special attention. She planned to wear it tonight with well-pressed jeans.

She took a quick shower when she'd finished. Putting on her clothes, she stared at her reflection in the long wardrobe mirror. There was a look of excitement in her eyes. Yes, she had to admit that she was really looking forward to spending the evening with Carl.

He intrigued her. The more she got to know him the more she liked him. He was fun to be with—except today when he'd snapped at her. But she could understand why. It was certainly true that she'd been lucky with her family background.

The sound of a car in the drive set her pulse racing. Carl was early and she wasn't ready. She leaned out of the window to see him trying to steer his car alongside hers. He climbed out and she called to him.

'I'll be down in a minute.'

He looked up at her. 'Not much room in your drive. I'd have left the car in the road if I'd known what a tight squeeze it was. However shall I get out?'

'You'll have to reverse. It's no problem.'

She closed the window, picked up her capacious shoulder-bag and checked that money, keys and tissues were on the top layer of the varied contents, before running down the stairs.

She smiled as she opened the door. Carl, in jeans and a casual sweater, was sitting on the stone bench seat in her little porch, his long legs sprawled across the flagstones, entirely blocking the way out.

'Nice place you've got here—apart from the impossible driveway.'

'It's not impossible if you've only got one car.'

He gave her a wry grin. 'Doesn't the maid have her own car?'

'Don't start that again!'

He pulled himself to his feet. 'Sorry. Couldn't resist it. Come on, let's go.'

'I'll go out to the road and make sure it's clear when you back out.'

When Carl emerged from the driveway Jenni climbed into his car.

'When I can get around to it I'm going to have a semicircular drive constructed so that cars can drive all the way round. But it's low down on my list of priorities.'

'So you've actually made a list. How organised! What's at the top?'

They were driving up the steep hill out of the valley. Reaching the summit, the road levelled out and ran between stretches of moorland.

She smiled to herself. 'Top of my list? Ah, that's a secret.'

'I think I've got a good idea,' he said quietly.

She glanced across at the firm set of his jaw, outlined against the setting sun. He was waiting for her to elaborate, but she remained silent as she weighed up the pros and cons of confiding in him.

'You weren't joking, were you, last week when we were going back to hospital after the wedding? About wanting a baby?'

She hesitated. 'No, I wasn't joking.'

'But have you thought of all the implications?'

'Of course I have! What do you take me for?'

She made an effort to modify her tone. 'My baby would want for nothing, either materially or emotionally. He'd be surrounded by a loving extended family— Grandma, Grandpa, eleven cousins at the present count, three aunts, three uncles. I've got my own house, money in the bank from Grandma's legacy. . .'

'Fine, you've convinced me. I'm not against the idea of single parents.'

'You're not?' She stared at him in surprise. 'Then why are you asking all these questions? I thought you disapproved or something.'

'No, I think it's a good idea.' His tone was bland, devoid of emotion.

She gave a sigh of relief. For some reason it had been very important to her that she should have Carl's approval. She was glad she'd taken the plunge and confided in him.

He pulled up in front of the Coach and Horses, an old pub set back from the moorland road. A couple of sheep wandered past as Jenni got out of the car. She breathed in the refreshing moorland air.

Inside they crossed the uneven, flagstoned floor to sit on an ancient wooden settle beside the smouldering log fire, placing their drinks on a well-grooved table. Jenni glanced around and was relieved to find that there were no hospital staff there.

The grapevine would be sure to start humming if she was seen out alone with the divine Carl! There was no such thing as a platonic relationship where some of the Moortown General crowd were concerned. The Coach and Horses was a favourite haunt after duty, but so far they'd been lucky.

'Hungry?' Carl asked her.

'Starving. What shall we have?'

She glanced across at the blackboard, propped up on the bar.

' "Today's specials," ' she read. 'Oh, that's for me! Home-made shepherd's pie.'

'I'll get two,' Carl said, going over to the bar.

The shepherd's pies were delicious. Jenni drank some more wine as she leaned back against the wooden settle at the end of their meal. The logs had been replenished, and flames were roaring up the wide chimney. She was feeling decidedly mellow.

'You were right, Carl.'

'About what?'

'I shouldn't have said that Madelaine Farrow was a bad mother. She's just been dealt a rotten deal, that's all. When I think of all my advantages it helps to put things in perspective.'

He reached across and squeezed her hand. 'Do you know something, Jenni, you're very sweet really. Not a bit like the dragon I thought you were.'

She smiled at him. 'But you shouldn't have snapped at me like that, even if I was sounding off a bit.'

His eyes held an enigmatic expression. 'No, I shouldn't. I didn't realise I'd still got a chip on my shoulder.'

'What do you mean?'

He let go of her hand and put his fingertips together, staring ahead as if he could see something she couldn't.

'You see, I didn't have all your advantages, Jenni, and sometimes it makes me mad when people who've always had everything going for them start criticising the less fortunate. I should have got over it by now but. . .'

He turned to look at her and she saw the pain in his dark brown eyes.

'Tell me about it,' she said quietly.

Carl glanced around them. In the background a radio was playing light classical music. Two farmers leaned against the bar. A middle-aged couple sat at a table at the other end of the pub. He seemed satisfied that they weren't going to be overheard.

'I never really got to know my parents. I remember that Sandra, my mother, was very beautiful.'

'You told me she had golden hair.'

He gave a sad smile. 'Yes, she did. She was an actress in a rep company. That's where she met my dad. He was managing the company and playing bit parts. They never made much money, just enough to get by. They were always busy, charging around from one town to the next. I don't know how they ever had time to produce me.'

'You were born in the proverbial suitcase,' Jenni said lightly, finding this serious side of Carl difficult to cope with.

'More or less. My grandmother told me that my mum took a week off and went to her flat in east London to have me. She was back on stage the next week and Grandma was literally left holding the baby, of which she never ceased to remind me.'

'So you weren't exactly the apple of your grand-mother's eye,' Jenni said gently.

'Oh, she did her best, but she was getting old and I was too much for her. Occasionally there would be rows if my mother called in when she was working nearby, mainly about money and how much it cost to feed and clothe me. Mum would put my clothes in a bag and storm out, taking me to go and live with her and my father. After that I was left by myself in all sorts of strange hotels and boarding-houses while my parents worked.'

'What about going to school?'

'As soon as I was five I was taken back to Grandma's flat so that I could go to the local primary school. I remember my mum begging Gran to take me in, promising more money—all the usual bribes to get rid of me.'

'How did you feel about being left with your Grandma again?'

'Feel?' He pulled a wry face. 'By the time I was five I'd taught myself that feelings were a luxury not to be indulged in if you wanted to avoid disappointment.'

He paused, running a hand through his hair—seemingly preparing to chose his words carefully. Jenni waited.

'That sounded a bit sanctimonious,' he said quietly. 'I don't want you to think I was sorry for myself. It was the only life I knew. As a little boy, I just lived from one minute to the next and tried to cope with whatever came along. Actually, going to school was a relief from the life I'd been leading. I enjoyed being with other children and then when I'd learned to read it was as if a whole new world had opened up to me.'

She swallowed hard. 'What made you decide to be a doctor?'

Again he studied the tips of his fingers, a faraway expression in his eyes. Jenni could see that he was reliving his difficult childhood, and her heart went out to him as she listened to the next part of his story.

'I remember standing in the casualty department in this big hospital in London. I was ten at the time. It was the middle of the night. Gran had got me out of bed to go with her. I didn't know why. There were bright lights everywhere. I thought it was all rather exciting. Then Gran went behind a screen. When she came out she was crying. A nurse took us both into a little room and gave Gran a cup of tea.'

'What had happened?' Jenni asked gently.

'My parents had been driving to London. It was foggy on the motorway, several cars ploughed into each other and they were unlucky.'

'Were they. . .?'

'Dad was killed outright. Mum survived and was still alive when we got to the hospital. They wouldn't let me go behind the screen to see her. The nurse said the doctors were very clever and would try to make Mum better. That was when I decided that I'd like to be a doctor.'

'And did your mother. . .?'

'No, Mum died about an hour later. I went back home with Gran. Gran died when I was sixteen, but I stayed on in her flat till after I was settled at medical school.'

'Carl, I'm sorry. I'd no idea you'd had such a hard time.'

'Of course you didn't. I've never told anybody before. I prefer to keep my past a secret.'

'We seem to be making a habit of telling each other our secrets,' she said quietly.

He put his hand over hers again. 'Now it's your turn. Enough of my sob-story. Tell me about this bright future that you're planning. We've established that you're financially sound, surrounded by a loving family and an expert in baby care. But there's just one small point you haven't explained.'

He paused, and a long slow smile spread across his handsome face.

'Which is?' she asked, knowing full well what he was going to say but playing for time.

'What are you going to do about finding a father for your baby?'

'I'm thinking of going down to Bramdale Clinic and speaking to Trish and Adam about the possibilities of artificial insemination.'

She spoke in a rush, anxious to get the idea over to him. She didn't want him to think that she was looking around for a suitable man. . .but then again. . .

That idea had certain advantages. And disadvantages too! Not least the fact that the father would want to become involved in the rearing of the child, and it was going to be her baby! No bossy men would complicate her life. She was going to keep hold of the reins, just like she did on Nightingale.

'Do you think Trish and Adam will be sympathetic towards your idea?' he asked evenly.

'I don't see why not. As we've already ascertained I've got the perfect situation for bringing up a baby. I'd have to pay for the AI treatment, of course.'

'There could be a simpler solution,' he said carefully.

She took a deep breath. 'Which is?'

'Well. . .'

He was looking towards the door. Two men and two girls were making their way towards the fire.

With a sinking feeling, Jenni recognised junior registrar Pete Jones. His fiery red hair was unmistakable. He was accompanied by Brian Hobbs, one of the housemen on Nightingale, and two of her junior nurses, dark-haired Tessa Manning and small, blonde Phoebe Sparks.

'Look who's here!' Pete Jones said. 'Mind if we join you?'

'Actually, we were just going,' Jenni said, reaching for her shoulder-bag.

Carl stood up. 'Who's holding the fort, Pete?'

'Georgina's got things under control, Carl. Everything was quiet when we left.'

A pale watery moon hung over the car park as they walked silently back to the car.

'I'll drop you off and go back to the hospital,' Carl said, opening the passenger door for Jenni. 'Georgina Cole's conscientious but she's not very experienced.'

'I agree,' Jenni said as Carl drove off down the moorland road in the direction of Cragdale. 'Georgina's a very junior, newly qualified doctor. I'm glad you're going back, Carl.'

She leaned back on the head-rest and closed her eyes, knowing that she was relieved Carl was going back to hospital on two counts. From a professional point of view, she wanted to make sure that her patients were in the hands of a senior doctor; on a personal level, she didn't want to have to discuss any more about how she was going to achieve her aim.

As she stole a glance, sideways, at Carl she saw that his jaw was set determinedly forward. It was as if he too was emotionally exhausted by their conversation. They'd poured out their hearts to each other and now they needed time to themselves. They were both very private people, unused to sharing secrets.

She wondered if he was already regretting being so open with her. And what was it that he'd been going to say to her when the Moortown crowd arrived?

CHAPTER THREE

For nearly three weeks Jenni tried to bring herself to make an appointment at the Bramdale clinic, but she kept convincing herself that she was too busy at the moment to see Trish and Adam.

Sitting on a nursing chair in the postnatal unit—feeding one of the babies—she looked out through the open window at the cloudless blue May sky. The sun was already warm; summer was just around the corner—a perfect time for taking the first steps towards her goal. So what was holding her back?

If she was honest with herself she would admit that it was Carl who'd blown her off course that night at the Coach and Horses when he'd started to say that there might be a simpler solution to artificial insemination. If Carl's solution was what she suspected then it wouldn't necessarily be simpler!

It was true that she worried about being matched with the right sperm donor. The unknown father of her baby would have to be intelligent and healthy.

But, then, the clinic would check all that out, wouldn't they? And the donor would remain anonymous. So why didn't she just get on with it?

The baby in her arms put her head back and stopped feeding.

'Come on, Stephanie,' Jenni coaxed. 'That's not enough breakfast for a growing girl like you.'

Gently she persuaded the little rosebud mouth to latch onto the bottle again. 'That's better.'

'She's so slow, isn't she, Sister?' Vicky Green, the baby's mother, arrived back from her morning bath. 'But she takes more from you than me.'

'You just have to keep nudging her along, Vicky,' Jenni said. 'She's beginning to gain weight but we'll have to be patient.'

'I'm just glad she's alive, Sister,' Vicky said.

'Yes, Stephanie's certainly a survivor,' Jenni said thankfully, as she remembered the first few days of the baby's life when the tiny prem battled for her life in an incubator. She'd been tube-fed for the first three weeks and had been a difficult feeder ever since.

'Madelaine's asking for you, Sister,' Nurse Tessa Manning said.

'Tell her I'll be along as soon as I've finished this feed, Nurse.'

As she burped the tiny baby over her shoulder Jenni was wondering how she was going to deal with Madelaine's problems. She couldn't keep mother and baby here indefinitely, but she couldn't turn her out until the social services had found her somewhere to stay. So far Madelaine had steadfastly refused all the options that had been put to her.

Madelaine was sitting on the bed, cradling her sleeping baby, when Jenni arrived in the cubicle.

'My boyfriend, Nick, just phoned me, Sister. His mum says she'll have us.'

Jenni knew she should be relieved but all she felt was apprehension. She looked down at the sleeping Jonathan. She couldn't let him leave here until she was satisfied that he was going to be well cared for.

'Do the social services know about this, Madelaine?'

The young mother shrugged. 'Not unless Nick's mum has told them, which is unlikely. She's not a bad old thing, really. Bit bossy but, then, that's mums for you, isn't it?'

'Is your own mum bossy?'

Madelaine pulled a wry face. 'She was before she took off and left me. Haven't seen her since I was eight.'

'And your dad?' Jenni prompted gently.

'Never knew him,' Madelaine said lightly.

Jenni looked down at little Jonathan and hoped that he wasn't going to suffer the same sort of life. She intended to do as much as she could for Madelaine.

'Has Nick's mum got room for you?' she asked.

'She's going to apply for a bigger house and then she will have.'

'But that could take ages!'

Madelaine grinned. 'I know. We'll just have to stay here, won't we, Sister? I like it here.'

'I know you do, Madeleine,' Jenni said, trying to stop the exasperation from creeping into her tone, 'but I can't keep you here indefinitely. We need your bed.'

'Just for a little while, eh?'

The young woman cocked her head on one side and gave a broad smile. 'Oh, here's Dr Devine. You'll back me up, won't you, Sister?'

Jenni looked up at Carl and smiled in spite of the frustration that she felt at this catch twenty-two situation.

'If it was up to me you could live here, Madelaine,' Carl said in a sympathetic tone, 'but we've got to think about all the other mums, queueing up to have their babies. We'll see what we can do for you.'

He looked at Jenni. 'I'm on my way to the gynae unit. I've just been bleeped about an emergency admission. I was told to bring you along with me.'

They hurried out into the corridor. Carl remained

silent on their way to the gynae unit. It wasn't simply that this was an emergency. Jenni had noticed that for the past three weeks, since their night out at the Coach and Horses, Carl's attitude towards her had been utterly professional.

It was almost as if he regretted telling her about his background. He'd shown the real, human Carl behind the carefree façade and she suspected that he wanted to regain his cool image.

Curtains were drawn around the new admission's bed. Pete Jones, their junior registrar, was examining the patient's abdomen, assisted by Staff Nurse Carol Thomas. They looked relieved when Carl and Jenni arrived.

Jenni took the young woman's hand. The skin was cold and clammy. Wide, frightened, tearful eyes stared up at her.

'I haven't lost the baby have I, Sister?' the patient said in a small voice.

'I hope not,' Jenni said gently, wishing that someone would quickly fill her in on the case details. Carl was already scanning the notes that had arrived with her.

'This is Mrs Patsy Appleyard, Sister,' Pete Jones said. 'She thinks she's about three months pregnant. She couldn't sleep last night because of pain in the abdomen.'

'Tell me where you feel the pain,' Carl said, placing his hands over the patient's abdomen.

Jenni could see that, although Carl was palpating very gently, Patsy Appleyard suffered pain when he touched the area over the lower right section of the abdomen. They looked at each other across the bed. Jenni could see that Carl was trying not to jump to conclusions.

'It could be appendicitis,' he said quietly to Jenni. 'On the other hand. . .'

'On the other hand, with a three-month pregnancy. . .'

Carl nodded. 'Exactly! I think we'd better do a laparoscopy and check the Fallopian tubes.'

He took hold of the patient's hand. 'We're going to take you along to Theatre, put you to sleep and check out what's going on.'

Carl was thinking, like Jenni, that it might be an ectopic pregnancy, where the foetus was developing in the Fallopian tube. They had to deal with the affected tube as quickly as possible. If it ruptured into the abdomen there would be unpleasant complications. But from the feel of the cold clammy skin and the rapid pulse they might already be too late.

Jenni prepared her patient for Theatre, while Carl went along to check that everything was ready for him. He phoned through to Nightingale to ask for his patient, and Staff Nurse Carol Thomas took Mrs Appleyard to Theatre.

A couple of hours went by during which Jenni was busily occupied with her normal duties on Nightingale, but her mind kept flitting away to think about her new patient. She wouldn't ring through to Theatre. Carl would keep her posted.

It was the middle of the afternoon before her patient returned. Carl walked alongside the theatre porters. He looked tired and decidedly dispirited.

'We were right,' he told Jenni quietly. 'It was an ectopic. We couldn't save the foetus. The tube had already ruptured, so Patsy will need some more blood when this bottle finishes. There are two more packs in the ward fridge. She's on antibiotics, which should deal with the infection in the abdomen.'

'Does she know anything about what's happened?'

'She's only just coming round. You can call me when she's fully conscious and I'll come and explain the sad news or. . .'

'That's OK. I'll speak to her when I think she can take it,' Jenni said.

He gave her a grateful smile. 'I hoped you might. This sort of thing comes better if it's woman to woman. I'm not very good at dealing with deep emotions.'

'Oh, I'm not sure about that,' Jenni said, softly.

For a moment his eyes flickered warily.

Once again her heart went out to this grown-up version of the unwanted little boy who'd deliberately stifled his emotions.

'When I've finished here this evening would you like to come out to the cottage for supper, Carl?' she heard herself saying.

'I'd enjoy that. I've got to go back to Theatre. I'll see you later.'

Patsy Appleyard was coming round, stirring fitfully and complaining about the pain in her tummy. Jenni administered a shot of pethidine.

Patsy's pulse was too rapid and her temperature too high. Jenni gave her the next dose of antibiotics. Patsy still hadn't reached the level of consciousness where she was asking questions about the outcome of her operation.

Jenni assigned Staff Nurse Penny Drew to stay by the bedside and report any change in condition, while she went off to supervise the dispensing of the medicines.

It was a couple of hours before Staff Nurse Drew asked Jenni to see Mrs Appleyard. She was now fully conscious, and asking about her operation.

Jenni sat down beside her patient and took hold of her hand. Quietly, she told Patsy that they hadn't been able to save the pregnancy. The tiny foetus had developed in the Fallopian tube, causing it to break open.

She stayed silently sympathetic while Patsy wept and clung to her hand.

'Will I be able to have another baby, Sister?' Patsy said, through her tears.

'There's no reason why not,' Jenni said gently. 'Your other Fallopian tube is healthy so the eggs from your ovaries can travel down to the womb.'

'I'm so tired.' Patsy closed her eyes.

'Of course you are. Try to rest now. There's always a nurse near at hand if you need anything.'

'Thanks, Sister. You've all been so kind. I. . .'

Patsy's voice trailed away as she drifted off to sleep again.

Jenni handed over to the night staff at eight o'clock. She was in the middle of giving them her report at the nurses' station when Carl came in through the swing doors. During the course of her busy session of duty she'd forgotten that she'd promised him supper. It had seemed like a good idea earlier in the afternoon, but now all she wanted to do was kick off her shoes and flop down on the sofa with a good book.

He went off down the ward to check on Patsy Appleyard. By the time he returned Jenni had finished her report. She picked up her shoulder-bag and went out through the swing doors with Carl, acutely aware that the night staff were watching this interesting scenario.

'The grapevine will be humming before morning!' Jenni said as they walked down the corridor.

Carl laughed. 'Every time I'm seen anywhere with a girl the grapevine hums. During the last month my name has been linked with several.'

'So I've heard,' she said wryly.

'I don't take any notice of rumours, Jenni.'

'Neither do I.'

She stopped outside the staff cloakroom.

'I'll meet you in the car park. I've got to change out of my uniform.'

In the cloakroom she pulled on jeans and a sweater. Feeling already more relaxed, she went out to the car park. Carl was standing by her car.

'Are you dead set on cooking, Jenni, or shall we pick up a take-away?' he asked.

She laughed. 'You must have been reading my mind. A take-away sounds good to me.'

'Indian? Chinese?'

They agreed on Indian, before driving off in convoy to call in at the take-away counter of the Raj Restaurant.

Driving down into Cragdale, Jenni glanced in the rear-view mirror. Carl was right behind her. She turned into her drive and he followed.

Although the house still held the latent heat of the warm spring day, Jenni gathered sticks and firelighters together.

'This isn't for the heat,' she told Carl. 'I like the cosy effect a fire has on my little sitting-room. It seems to make it more friendly.'

Carl smiled. 'Let me make the friendly fire while you dish out the curry.'

They sat on the rug in front of the tentative flames

and dug their forks into the foil containers, spread out between them.

'Wow, the curry's hot,' Jenni said, taking a sip from her can of beer to soothe her tingling tongue.

Carl leaned across, holding out one of the containers.

'Try some of this mango chutney, designed to cool you down in a hot climate. And chew on a poppadom before they lose their snap and crackle.'

She leaned back against the sofa at the end of their impromptu meal, surrounded by the debris of paper and containers, and looked into the fire where the flames were now leaping up the chimney.

She smiled. 'I'm glad you didn't want me to serve this on my best bone china dinner service.'

Carl laughed. 'It's a good thing you didn't try to stand on ceremony. I was far too hungry. I think I forgot to have lunch.'

'Me too! Would you like coffee?'

He nodded. 'Let me clear the table, ma'am.'

Jenni prepared the cafetière while Carl gathered up the debris in a large plastic bag and dumped it in the kitchen bin.

Returning to the sitting-room with coffee and cups, Jenni felt suddenly uncharacteristically shy. In the flurry of the activity of their meal she hadn't had time to consider what they might do afterwards. Would Carl want to watch TV, listen to music perhaps?

She slotted a CD into her player and the haunting strains of Mendelssohn's violin concerto wafted over them.

'I like this,' Carl murmured, leaning back against the cushions of the sofa.

As she handed him a cup of coffee she wondered if he was referring to the music or the general relaxed ambience of their evening. It was both, as far as she was concerned. She chose the armchair nearest to the fire and curled her legs underneath her.

Carl looked across at her. 'So, what did Trish and Adam have to say about your proposal? Are you booked into the Bramdale clinic yet?'

She lowered the volume of the music. 'You certainly ask direct questions, Carl.'

He smiled. 'And direct questions require direct answers. You left me in no doubt about how determined you were to go ahead so I'm simply asking. . .'

'I haven't got around to it yet.'

'Why?'

'Because I haven't had time. I've had a million things on my mind. With a full-time job and the cottage to take care of, there's barely time to. . .'

'You're stalling, aren't you? My diagnosis is that you're suffering from a severe case of procrastination.'

His tone was gentle but his eyes probed her face.

She sighed. 'How did you know?'

Because, from what I've seen of you, Jenni, you're a very determined character and if you want something you'll move heaven and earth to get it. So, what's the problem?'

She hesitated. 'I've been worrying about getting the right sperm donor. I know the Bramdale clinic has a good reputation. They'll only inseminate with first-class sperm, specially selected and matched. . .'

'Jenni, I've told you there's an easier way.'

She hesitated. 'I remember you started to tell me when we were out at the Coach and Horses.'

She stood up and put another log on the fire to hide her flushed cheeks.

'The natural method poses no problems,' he continued in a cool, analytical voice. 'The mother knows who the father is and therefore every facet of the baby's genetic make-up can be checked out in advance.'

'But the mother would have to put up with the father for the rest of her child's life,' she said quietly.

'Not necessarily, not if the mother chooses carefully. Not every man wants to be saddled with a child.'

He paused. Jenni waited. Their eyes met. He smiled.

'What I'm getting at is this,' he continued. 'If you'd like me to help you I will, and I wouldn't want anything to do with the end product.'

She stared at him, for once at a loss for words. When she'd recovered her equilibrium she said, 'You mean you'd offer yourself as a sperm donor and you wouldn't even want to see the child?'

'That's what I said. I'm moving on from Moortown at the end of October so I won't be around.'

She leaned back in her chair, knowing that this was what she'd been holding out for. She wanted to be able to visualise her baby's father. And in the years to come Carl's handsome face and athletic build would certainly be a joy to conjure up. And if her baby was a boy he would have Carl's good looks.

He leaned across and touched the arm of her chair. 'Why are you staring at me like that?'

She flushed deeper. 'No reason.'

'You were worrying about the method, weren't you?'

'Method?' She knew her voice sounded squeaky.

'Look, Jenni, we're both mature adults. It's possible for two intelligent people with our medical training to look upon this as a conception operation. Conceiving by the natural method will be easier, and you can do away with all the red tape and examinations that would be required by the Bramdale clinic.'

'Not to mention the expense,' Jenni put in quickly, as she found herself warming to the idea. 'But, then, I don't see why you should offer your services for free, Carl. You must let me. . .'

'Oh, don't be silly, Jenni,' he smiled. 'This is an arrangement between friends. It will be my pleasure.'

They looked at each other and laughed. 'That was an unfortunate choice of words,' Carl said. 'But you know what I mean. So, do you want to take me up on my offer?'

'Absolutely!' She held out her hand to shake on their agreement.

He took hold of her hand in both of his, smiling into her eyes. 'We'll finalise the details later.'

'But not tonight,' she said in a small, slightly panicky voice. 'I need to check when it would be the best time of the month and. . .'

'Of course. Take your time, Jenni. I'm in no rush. It's your baby.'

Yes, it would be her baby! She smiled as she thought what a perfect arrangement this was going to be. What a wonderful man Carl was! She'd been so lucky to have met him just at the right time. It was as if fate had sent him along to help create her dream.

She stared into the fire, willing herself not to look across at him again. He looked so handsome in the firelight. This gratitude she was feeling for him was turning into full-blown admiration. She would have to hang onto her feelings when they actually. . .when they actually. . .

She couldn't bring herself to think about what Carl had called the conception operation. One step at a time.

'I'll check my diary,' she said evenly, diving into

her shoulder-bag. 'It's down here somewhere amongst all this junk.'

He seemed amused by her embarrassment. 'Like I said, there's no rush.'

'Well, if you're going off in October we'd better get a move on. It may not take the first time and. . .'

'That's OK. There'll be no problem about a second operation. Let's see, it's the middle of May now so we've got June, July, August. . .'

'Where are you going when you leave Moortown in October?' she asked quickly, trying not to think about the long summer months when she would be trying to conceive a baby with this very disturbing man. She was trying not to admit to herself that she might enjoy the experience.

'Oh, didn't I tell you? I'm going to be medical director of Gold Star Cruise Line.'

'Wow! What a fantastic job! How did you manage to get it?'

'I was a doctor on several ships for a number of years before I went back to work in the hospital in London where I'd trained. I started again at thirty as a junior registrar, worked up to senior registrar and then decided it was time to move on again. So I applied to Gold Star and got the post, starting in November.'

'I can see you suffer from the itchy feet syndrome.'

He smiled. 'You could say that.'

'So, Moortown General is just a stop-gap, is it?'

'I saw the temporary post advertised in a medical journal and I could see it would be ideal for me. The only thing was that I hadn't a clue where Moortown was. But everyone's been so friendly, especially you, Jenni. Do you know, I think I value our friendship more than anything at the moment?'

He stood up and moved to put his hands on the arm of her chair. The smile on his face was tender as he leaned towards her and kissed her cheek.

She held her breath as the light-as-a-feather experience ended. She could feel a turmoil of emotions deep down inside her. She wished he hadn't kissed her. . .but she was glad he had!

He was pulling away from her, returning to the sofa and sprawling his long legs over the rug.

'Better check our diaries,' Jenni said, riffling through the pages as she told herself that, whatever she did, she mustn't become emotionally involved with Carl. The conception of her baby had to be a purely medical experience.

She looked across and saw that he was studying her minutely.

'How about the twelfth of June?' she said quickly.

He looked down at the black leather book on his lap. 'Looks fine. In the evening?'

'Yes. . .er. . .you'd better come here, Carl.'

He smiled. 'Well, I hadn't planned on inviting you down to the residents' quarters.'

He was hauling himself to his feet.

'I'd better get back and see how things are going on Nightingale.'

'Will you check on Patsy Appleyard for me? Night Sister Maggie Warren is fairly new to the job so I want to be sure that she's thorough.'

'Don't worry, I'll keep her on her toes for you. Thanks for the supper, Jenni.'

'Don't thank me—it was you who insisted on paying,' she said as she led the way to her front door.

'Ah, but it was you who provided the cosy cottage and all the necessary trimmings for a great evening.'

He was leaning against the door, his hand on the wall above her head. She tried to avoid looking into his eyes, which were too near for comfort. She could feel her pulse beginning to race, and found herself wondering how on earth she would cope with their next meeting here!

They were being so polite with each other, both aware of the wheels they'd set in motion. She realised that that was how their friendship must stay. Polite, considerate, devoid of emotion.

She looked up and swallowed hard as she saw the tender expression in his eyes.

'Goodnight, Jenni,' he said softly, bending forward to kiss her on the cheek.

She leaned against the door after he'd gone and her hand stole up to the side of her face where she'd experienced the touch of Carl's lips.

She mustn't allow herself to be so profoundly moved by a simple goodnight kiss between friends! Carl meant nothing to her other than a means to an end, she told herself firmly.

But as she climbed the stairs she knew that it wasn't going to be easy to ignore the deep attraction she was beginning to feel towards him.

CHAPTER FOUR

JENNI was very busy on Nightingale for the next couple of weeks. In her off-duty she found time to go home to see her parents a couple of times, but apart from that she'd simply flitted between her Cragdale cottage and hospital.

She hadn't seen Carl in her off-duty time. He hadn't even suggested that they go out for a drink together and she told herself that she was glad. They were both making the effort to remain detached about their arrangement for the twelfth of June. But as the day approached Jenni found herself becoming more and more apprehensive.

Once, waking in the dead of night, she felt she couldn't go through with it. It would be so difficult to regard it as a clinical operation. She would have to tell Carl that she was having second thoughts.

But when the sun peeped over her window-sill in the morning her spirits revived. She told herself that she would simply concentrate on why she was putting herself through all this.

She would love a baby! A child of her own—loved, wanted—to be given every chance in life, to be drawn into the emotional warmth of her family.

On the actual day she was again having cold feet about the proposed conception operation. So when Carl breezed into her office, behind the nurses' station, her heart started pounding.

'All set for tonight?' he asked, a friendly smile firmly fixed to his face.

She swallowed. 'Yes. And you?'

'Of course.'

'Carl. . .' She glanced nervously around her empty office, before fixing her eyes on the door that might open at any second to allow inquisitive medical personnel to hear her.

'Carl, you haven't mentioned our arrangement to anyone, have you?'

He moved closer, a sympathetic expression on his face. 'Of course I haven't!' He put his hands on her shoulders and looked down at her.

She was reassured by the understanding expression in his eyes. It was going to be OK.

'Now, stop worrying. It's the most natural thing in the world. I'll come round about eight-thirty and. . .'

'Make it nine,' she cut in. 'I can't leave here till after eight and. . .'

The door was opening. Staff Nurse Rona Phillips stood on the threshold, smiling as she looked from Carl to Jenni.

The queen of the grapevine! Jenni thought. Trust Rona to come in at the most inopportune moment.

'What can I do for you, Rona?'

'I've brought a couple of your ex-patients up from Outpatients. Sally Fowlds and Jean Crabtree have been in for their appointments with Simon Delaware, and they were asking if they could come up to see you, Sister. I said I'd see if it was convenient.'

Jenni smiled as she recovered her professional equilibrium.

'Of course. I'd love to see them.'

'They're waiting outside at the nurses' station.'

'Well, send them in, Rona.' She looked at Carl. 'Have you time to stay and see them, Carl?'

He nodded. 'I was going to ask Simon how those two were getting along since we discharged them.'

Rona showed in the two ex-patients.

'Lovely to see you both,' Jenni said. 'Come and sit down and tell us how you're getting on.'

She remembered that Sally and Jean had become firm friends while they were on Nightingale.

'It was a good thing you introduced me to Jean, Dr Devine,' Sally said. 'I was hell-bent on getting rid of my womb but you told me how Jean had suffered with early menopause and you changed my mind for me. That device you fixed in my womb has done the trick, Doctor. There was no flooding at all when my period came.'

'That's what I'd hoped,' Carl said. 'And how are you, Jean? Is the hormone replacement therapy helping?'

'It certainly is. I'm feeling on top of the world. I was feeling so frisky I chased my old man round the bedroom last night.'

Carl smiled. 'And did you catch him?'

Jean giggled. 'Oh, yes. He didn't put up much resistance. The physiotherapists told me to get plenty of exercise to ease my joints so it was just what I needed.'

'I can see you're a model patient, Jean, doing everything you've been told to do,' Carl said.

Everybody laughed. Carl looked at Jenni. 'I must get on, Sister. I'll be with you for the operation this evening.'

Jenni could feel the colour mounting in her cheeks as Carl prepared to leave.

'You doctors and nurses have to work so hard, don't

you?' Sally said. 'I suppose you do operations at all kinds of unsocial hours.'

'We take it all in our stride,' Carl said, his eyes twinkling with amusement as he looked at Jenni.

As Carl went towards the door dark-haired Staff Nurse Carol Thomas came in.

'Madelaine wants to say goodbye to you, Sister, and to you, Dr Devine. She's all ready to go home.'

'We'd better leave you to get on, Sister,' Jean said.

Carl and Jenni found Madelaine sitting on the edge of her bed, holding baby Jonathan in her arms. Jenni was pleased to see that Madelaine had dressed her baby in a warm all-in-one suit.

Even though it was now June, Jenni had impressed on Madelaine that she must insulate her baby from draughts and cool winds. Jonathan had spent the first weeks of his life cocooned in Nightingale's regulated temperature. He needed cotton-wool treatment for his first venture into the great outdoors.

When Madelaine had told Jenni, a week ago, that her boyfriend, Nick, had rented a caravan on the cliffs, near the seaside town of Filey, Jenni had immediately contacted the social services and told them of her fears for the baby's welfare. But she had been assured that the young family would be closely monitored. Trained professionals would visit to check that all was well.

So now, as Jenni looked down at baby Jonathan, she tried to put aside her worries for him. It wasn't her problem any more. She was handing him over.

Madelaine held out her hand and took hold of Jenni's.

'Thanks for everything, Sister. You've been great. A bit bossy sometimes.'

She grinned, looking up at Jenni, her eyes full of affection.

'It goes with the job, Madelaine,' Carl said. 'It's all on the surface. Sister's quite soft-hearted when you get to know her.'

'I know,' Madelaine said, her voice suddenly croaky. 'Well, can't stay here any longer. Nick's waiting for me downstairs.'

Jenni leaned forward and gently kissed baby Jonathan. Not a very professional thing to do but where babies were concerned she tended to act with her heart, not her head.

'Come back and see us, won't you, Madelaine?'

'If you ever want a trip to the seaside come and see us, Sister. You too, Doctor,' Madelaine said, standing up.

'Thank you. Let me get one of the nurses to carry Jonathan for you,' Jenni said quickly, as she watched Madelaine reaching for one of her bags. Once Jonathan was safely off the hospital premises she could, theoretically, stop worrying about him.

As their patient went off down the ward, turning to wave from the door, Carl said to Jenni, 'See you tonight. Nine o'clock.'

She took a deep breath. 'Would you like supper. . .before. . .?'

He grinned. 'Only if you insist.'

She gave him a nervous smile. 'Oh, I do.'

'What you mean is we need to keep up our strength, don't you?'

'From a medical point of view, yes.'

Their eyes met and she felt the unnerving pull of attraction towards him. It wouldn't be any hardship to find herself close to Carl! She knew, without a shadow of a doubt, that this was the worrying factor about tonight's so-called operation. She didn't know how she was going to get through it without losing her cool—

without displaying some of the unwelcome emotions that were already confusing her.

It was an effort to concentrate on her duties for the rest of the day. Carl was in Theatre all afternoon so she didn't see him again.

In the early evening she had to spend a couple of hours in her mother and baby unit, helping with feeding problems and giving advice to the new mums, but she always found this part of her work very rewarding.

As she dimmed the lights in the baby unit one of the mothers called out, 'Going anywhere nice tonight, Sister?'

'Home to bed,' she replied, and felt the churning of her emotions.

'A young woman like you should be going out on the town,' another patient called.

Jenni smiled. 'I'm not complaining. I enjoy a quiet night in.'

'Depends who's with you, doesn't it?'

Jenni beat a hasty retreat before she could be asked any leading questions. She gave her report and handed over to Sister Maggie Warren, feeling pleased that the new night sister was proving to be conscientious. She had no worries about handing over the reins tonight.

In fact, she told herself as she walked out to her car, she had no worries about the evening ahead.

She put a match to the fire she'd already prepared as soon as she arrived home. The flames quickly sprang to life and took away the chill from the sitting-room. The calendar indicated that it was June, but a cold, northerly wind was blowing down from the moors and Jenni wanted the cottage to feel cosy when Carl arrived.

The home-made chicken casserole she'd removed from the freezer before going on duty was fully thawed.

She put it in the oven, before running upstairs for a quick shower.

What should she wear? At this point the reality of what she was about to do hit her with full force! Even regarding it as a clinical operation, she would still have to take her clothes off, well, some of them anyway. But she didn't want to wear something that shouted seduction!

In the end she chose jeans and a blue sweater—easy to put on, easy to take off.

The sound of tyres, crunching on the stones outside, sent her hurtling down the stairs again, only to stem her enthusiasm as she reached the front door. Mustn't seem too excited, even though her heart was beating extraordinarily fast. Stay calm, she told herself. Don't become emotionally involved—this is simply a means to an end.

'Hi!' She smiled as she opened the door.

Carl was wearing jeans and a blue sweater, just like she was.

'We look like twins,' she said.

'Great minds think alike. Obviously this is the garb to be worn for clinical operations of this nature. I've brought the pre-operative medication.'

Jenni smiled as she looked at the bottle of champagne he was holding. 'Are you sure we've been written up for that?'

'Absolutely! It's designed to effect perfect relaxation which, as you know, is one of the pre-requisites for success in this kind of operation.'

'Oh, well, in that case I'll find the medicine glasses.'

When she returned to the sitting-room with a couple of champagne glasses she found Carl stretched out on the sofa in front of the fire.

'I'm glad you lit the fire,' he said as he removed the cork and poured out the champagne. 'It's important to keep the patients warm. Cheers! Here's to a successful operation!'

She sat down on the sofa and clinked her glass against Carl's. Their eyes met. She took a sip of her champagne and then another one.

'That's a delicious smell, wafting in from your kitchen,' Carl said.

Jenni smiled. 'It's a good thing we don't have to administer a general anaesthetic, otherwise I'd have been forced to starve you.'

Carl's eyes twinkled merrily. 'This is one of those operations where we need active participation by the patients so an anaesthetic would be out of the question.'

Jenni gave a nervous laugh. 'Not even an epidural to numb the lower section of the body, Doctor?'

'Absolutely not! Sensations are very important in this operation.'

'I'll go and check on the casserole,' Jenni said quickly, carrying her champagne glass into the kitchen. She took another sip and told herself to stay calm as she placed the casserole on the kitchen table.

'Supper is served,' she called.

Carl came through to the kitchen and topped up her champagne glass.

'This is a seriously good casserole,' he said. 'I can honestly say that I don't mind how often we have to repeat this operation if it means you'll feed me every time.'

The medical banter continued throughout the meal. Jenni felt as if she were rehearsing for a part in a play. But as she put the empty casserole dish in the sink she acknowledged that this was no rehearsal. This was the real thing! Time to go upstairs and get on with the operation.

She cleared her throat. 'Would you like to use the bathroom, Carl? It's at the top of the stairs. I'll be up in a minute when I've put this dish in to soak.'

'How about the washing-up?' he said.

For the first time this evening she could tell that Carl was nervous too. He'd hidden behind the make-believe façade and now, when it came to the crunch, he was probably wishing he'd never volunteered his services.

'Oh, I'll leave them soaking and do them later,' she said, without turning round, as she ran water into the sink.

She heard him climb the stairs, go into the bathroom and the sound of water splashing. Was he taking a shower? Better give him time to get ready.

She stood at the foot of the stairs and took a deep breath. Two glasses of champagne had initially taken the edge off her shyness but now she felt stone cold sober and very nervous. As she climbed the stairs she told herself to relax.

He was coming out of the bathroom, one of her large bath towels draped around him. His torso was tanned. Dark hairs grew down the centre of his muscular chest, disappearing into the recesses of the towel. His upper arms were strong and firm, bulging with muscles.

She caught her breath, trying desperately to hide the admiration she was feeling at the sight of his athletic body.

'Carl, I didn't recognise you with your clothes off,' she quipped.

'Hope you don't mind me borrowing this towel. I should have brought a dressing-gown. Next time. . .'

'If there is a next time. . .I mean, I'm hoping I'll

conceive first time,' she said, her words tumbling out breathlessly. 'That's my bedroom. Go and. . .make yourself comfortable. I'll be with you in a minute.'

She went into the bathroom, shut the door and leaned against it, closing her eyes. If she was nervous how must Carl be feeling? Probably petrified!

Oh, she should have gone down to the Bramdale Clinic. Whatever had possessed her to go along with this mad idea? But it was too late to back out now.

She stripped off her clothes and climbed in the shower. She'd already had one shower this evening but she'd have another for good measure. She knew she was procrastinating. Carl would be waiting for her. . .in her bed.

She stepped on to the fluffy bathmat and pulled a clean towel from the cupboard. Her dressing-gown was in the bedroom so she chose the largest towel she could find. Draping it around her like a sarong, she looked in the mirror.

Long blonde hair cascaded over her naked shoulders, pink nail polish shone on her toes and her lightly tanned legs peeped out from the bottom of the towel. Oh, God, she looked exactly as if she was arranging a seduction scene!

She took a deep breath and told herself to stay cool and calm—ignore any sensations, ignore all emotions—it was a clinical operation. Just get it over with!

Carl was sitting up in bed, reading her latest copy of the *Nursing Times*. His dark hair was still damp and messed up from the shower. She couldn't deny that he looked heart-rendingly appealing!

'I'm reading about the statistics concerning infertile couples. Did you know that the overall success rate for women who undertake IVF treatment is considerably less than thirty per cent?'

'Yes, it's pretty low, isn't it?'

'Which points to the fact that the natural method of conception is still the most successful.'

She hovered beside the bed. . .her bed! Why didn't she just climb in? Perhaps she should slip on her nightdress?

He put down the *Nursing Times* and his eyes seemed to linger an awfully long time over her before he said, 'Would you like to join me? I was just thinking that the only thing missing in this delightfully comfy bed is a hot-water bottle. Failing that, I'll have to settle for a warm-blooded woman.'

'I'm afraid my feet are cold,' Jenni said as she climbed into bed, dropping her towel on the bedroom carpet and securing the duvet around her neck.

'Ouch! So they are,' he said as he pulled her towards him.

She could feel the hairs on his arms as he held her against him. His chest felt hard and unyielding; his thighs were now touching hers. The close contact with his skin was arousing feelings she'd hoped to avoid.

'You'd better relax, Jenni,' he said, 'otherwise conception will be a clinical impossibility. If I caress you very gently like this. . .'

His hands were stroking her with exquisite tenderness. She held her breath. Not only was she becoming relaxed but she was becoming hopelessly aroused and stimulated. She felt warm, moist and actually longing for the act that was required for her baby's conception. And as Carl held her tightly against him it was patently obvious from his hard arousal that he would have no problem with the essential part of the operation!

'I think I'm ready, Carl,' she whispered as she desperately tried to disguise her feelings.

She moved to accommodate him and he slipped inside her. The steady thrusting rhythm was moving her to feelings of delicious ecstasy. It was impossible to disguise her feelings any longer. Her body seemed to melt as they fused together, and she had no control over the cry that escaped her lips as her sensations turned into a tremendous climax.

As the sensations died down she could feel embarrassment creeping over her. She'd been so utterly abandoned as she'd participated. The whole experience had been mind-blowingly wonderful. She hadn't been able to disguise how much she'd enjoyed it.

She tried to move away but Carl's arms were firmly around her.

'Lie still,' he whispered.

Jenni was surprised and moved by the huskily tender tone of his voice. There was no need to feel embarrassed. He'd made it quite clear that he was enjoying it too.

'Some medical opinion holds that if the woman lies still after intercourse there's a better chance she'll conceive,' he said.

She tried to ignore the feel of his warm breath on her hair.

'Yes, at this very moment all your little spermatozoa will be swimming around, trying to fertilise my egg, won't they?'

'Fascinating thought,' he said quietly.

And then he bent his head and kissed her, oh, so gently, on the lips. It was strange to be lying there after having intercourse with Carl and yet finding that one kiss so moving. He raised his head and looked down at her. She saw the tender expression in his eyes.

'I would say that this has been a very successful operation,' he said gently.

Oh, God! Who were they trying to fool? It had been fantastic! She wanted to tell him how much she'd enjoyed being with him, but that wasn't part of the operation. Once Carl had made her pregnant the arrangement would cease.

'We shan't know how successful for a couple of weeks at least,' Jenni said, suddenly trying to make her voice sound very prim and proper and failing miserably. She was sure she hadn't fooled Carl.

'You'll let me know if you're pregnant as soon as you can, Jenni, won't you?'

'Of course. I hope we've been successful.'

He put his finger under her chin and lifted it so that she had to look into his eyes. 'Well, it'll be no hardship to have a repeat performance.'

'Do you think I've been lying still long enough?' she asked quickly, as she experienced definite feelings of desire stirring deep down inside her. If she stayed close to Carl much longer she would start to instigate the repeat performance now!

'Yes, I think the patient can get up now,' he said as he leaned back against the pillows, his eyes languidly tender.

'I'll make some coffee when you come down,' she said as she pulled on her dressing-gown.

'Thanks.' He was once more engrossed in the *Nursing Times*.

She went into the bathroom and stood in the shower again. Her skin was damp with perspiration. Mine and Carl's all mixed together, she thought as she raised her head to the cascade of hot water. Not to mention the precious little spermatozoa, swimming around inside her. Had one of them connected yet? She certainly felt different already.

But that could be for a totally different reason! She'd had a couple of meaningful relationships but she'd never experienced love-making like this before. There! She'd thought of it as love-making, and she was trying so hard to think of it in a cool, clinical, detached way.

She dried herself and put on her jeans and sweater. Carl's clothes, neatly folded, were on top of the bathroom chest. He would be waiting for her to come out so that he could get dressed.

She went down into the kitchen, made a large cafetière of coffee and carried it through into the sitting-room. The logs were still smouldering but only just. Carefully she rebuilt the fire, put a CD into her player and curled up on the sofa, cradling the coffee-cup in her hand.

She turned to look at Carl as he came down the open staircase at the side of the sitting-room. His hair was still messed up and the determined jaw thrust forward, accentuating his full, sensual lips. She remembered his kiss. . .

'Coffee?' she said hastily.

He smiled. 'Thanks. I'd love some. It's thirsty work, making babies.'

'Yes, but it's worth it. . .I mean. . .'

He laughed. 'Oh, Jenni, I do. . .I do enjoy being with you.'

She swallowed. 'Yes, I enjoy being with you too.'

He sat down on the sofa, took a sip of his coffee, put it down on the small occasional table and turned towards her.

She could feel an electric current running directly

between them as their eyes met. She was keeping a
tight rein on her emotions but it wasn't easy.

'I think maybe I'd better be getting back,' he said,
his voice unusually husky.

She stood up, as if to help him along his way. The
tension between them was palpable. They'd shared a
breathtaking experience. It wouldn't do to dwell on it.
It was best not to prolong their evening together. After
all, this was purely a clinical arrangement. Emotions
shouldn't come into it.

'Yes, you'd better go and check on the night staff,'
she said evenly, as she moved swiftly towards the front
door and started to fiddle with the locks. Suddenly her
fingers were all thumbs.

'Here, let me do that for you.'

He leaned across her from behind, his hard chest
dangerously close as he slid back the bolt, undid the
chain and turned the key in the lock.

'It's like Fort Knox!' he joked, his hand on the
half-open door.

She smiled. 'A woman on her own can't be too
careful.'

'And when you have a baby you'll have to be even
more careful,' he said, smiling down at her.

'Ah, won't it be wonderful?'

'Keep on reminding yourself how wonderful it will
be during the months ahead, Jenni. It could take a while
so you mustn't count your chickens.'

'Oh, I'm sure it's been successful. I feel different
already.'

'Do you? So do I,' he said quietly. 'Goodnight, Jenni.'

He kissed her gently on the lips. She found herself
savouring the moment. As she closed the door she told

herself that it had only been a moment—a goodnight kiss from a good friend who was trying to help her achieve her dream.

CHAPTER FIVE

As JENNI went about her routine tasks in the mother and baby unit—helping a mother to feed, chatting to a worried mother who needed reassurance, cuddling a baby until he stopped crying—she felt unusually detached from the scene. Usually she enjoyed this part of her morning, but today she had something on her mind that wouldn't go away.

Her period had arrived that morning. What a let-down after two weeks of hoping that she was pregnant! She lifted the baby from her lap to her shoulder, placed the bottle on a table and proceeded to gently pat and rub on his spine as she coaxed away the wind that had built up during his feed.

'Come on, Robert, just a little burp for Sister,' she murmured absently as her thoughts returned to her problem.

Her main problem today was that she would have to tell Carl that their operation had been unsuccessful. She'd promised to let him know the outcome as soon as possible. She knew that he would offer his services in a repeat performance but how could she possibly take him up on that, knowing how moved she'd been by their last encounter? She couldn't pretend again that she had no feelings for him.

Baby Robert gave a loud burp.

'There's a good boy,' Jenni said in a soothing voice. 'Now, shall we let Mummy change you?'

Diane, the young mother who had been watching Jenni, took hold of her baby.

'Stay with me, Sister. I want to get it right this time.'

Jenni remained for reassurance. First babies could be a problem to inexperienced mothers. Diane was unusually nervous. She'd had a difficult pregnancy and labour and had found it impossible to breast-feed. She was also very weak and needed to build up her strength.

Jenni glanced at Diane's chart as the young mother carefully arranged her son on the changing-mat and began to undo his nappy with shaky, inexperienced fingers.

'You must eat all the food that the diet kitchen sends for you, Diane,' Jenni said. 'You'll need all your strength to cope with young Robert when you get home.'

Diane nodded. 'I'll try, Sister. Can you hold Robert's legs still while I wash his bottom? Which cream do I put on afterwards? Is it this one or. . .' Her voice trailed away.

Jenni glanced up to see Simon Delaware arriving through the door. Obviously the sight of her consultant had put young Diane into a flap.

'You finish it, Sister,' the young mother whispered.

Simon smiled down at his patient. 'How are you getting on, Diane?'

'I'm fine. When can I go home, Mr Delaware?'

'As soon as you're fully recovered, Diane. A couple of days more should do the trick. Have you been taking your iron tablets?'

'Yes.'

'That's good.'

'Have you come to do a round?' Jenni asked Simon.

'I'd like to do one in a few minutes,' he said. 'I've

got a new batch of medical students, waiting outside. They're the first year ones who start in September. Most of them are straight from school. Would you mind if I took them round Nightingale?'

Jenni smiled. 'Please, go ahead. We've got to help our next generation of doctors.'

'Thanks. If you could possibly spend the time to come around with us, Sister. . .'

'Of course.'

Simon flashed her a grateful smile, before leaving the mother and baby unit. She saw baby Robert safely back in his cot, before going back to her office.

Rolling down her sleeves and fixing her starched cuffs in place, she glanced in the mirror. From her deliberately calm, ultra-professional expression no one could tell that she was trying to come to a difficult decision: AI treatment versus another session with Carl. What was it to be?

The door opened. 'There's a whole load of students out there, Sister, with Mr Delaware,' the diminutive, blonde-haired Penny Drew said. 'They look so young. I bet most of them are only eighteen.'

'I'm just coming, Penny.'

Simon Delaware's eyes registered relief when Jenni appeared. Surrounded by seven young men and three girls in regulation white coats, he looked uncharacteristically harassed.

'You have to remember that this is a working ward,' he was saying. 'Sister has very kindly allowed us to go round it, but you must be as quiet as possible and try not to disturb the patients. First, we're going to take a look at the obstetrics unit.'

Jenni walked ahead with Simon, and the group followed in silence. She decided that the students were being either dutifully quiet or completely overawed by the sight of heavily pregnant patients in various stages of labour.

As the round progressed one student in particular intrigued her. He was constantly asking Simon questions. She could see that he was very keen to learn. As they moved through into the postnatal section she found that the young man was standing next to her. She glanced up at him and was immediately taken by the colour of his hair. Dark brown, almost black, with a hint of gold running through it.

The only person she'd ever met with hair that colour was Carl. As if sensing that he was the object of her scrutiny, the young student turned to look at Jenni.

She did a double-take! Those dark brown expressive eyes, the thrust of the jaw. It was as if she was looking at a younger version of Carl. She turned away, telling herself that she'd become obsessed by Carl. She really must try to put him out of her mind.

As if on cue, the double doors swung open and the man himself walked down the ward. She could feel her pulse racing. He looked so handsome in his dove-grey suit, partially covered by a white coat. The dark, unruly hair that had been so messed-up during that moving experience two weeks ago was now slicked back into place. He looked every inch the experienced, calm professional.

He looked across the heads of the students who separated them and smiled. She smiled back. What was she going to tell him when they finally found themselves alone?

'Ah, Dr Devine,' Simon said. 'I'm glad you could join us. Would you like to explain the problems our patient has encountered?'

Carl moved through the throng of students to the bedside. Jenni saw him smiling down at the young, petite, auburn-haired patient in the bed. The patient smiled back warmly, obviously captivated by her doctor.

'This is Jillie Hill. She suffers from cephalopelvic disproportion. Has anyone any idea what that might be?'

The intriguing young man beside Jenni said, 'Yes, I've read about that, sir. It's when the maternal pelvis is too small to allow the passage of the foetal head.'

'That's right. And do you know how we would deal with it?'

'The safest method is Caesarean section,' the young man replied.

Carl nodded. 'That's exactly what I did.'

They moved on through the postnatal ward to visit the premature babies' unit, before briefly visiting the gynaecology unit.

Returning to the nurses' station at the end of the round Simon asked if any of the students were intending to specialise in obstetrics and gynaecology.

'Too early to say, sir,' said the keen, dark-haired young man, 'but I may do.'

'Well, at least I hope your visit to Nightingale hasn't put you off,' Jenni said.

The young man smiled. 'Quite the reverse.' He lowered his voice. 'Sister, do you think I might have a word with you in private?'

'Of course.'

Simon and his protégés were disappearing through the door. Carl was checking charts at the nurses' station. Sooner or later she would have to take him on one side and tell him the news. But for the moment she could spare a few minutes for this enthusiastic young student.

She closed the door of her office behind them. 'So you are. . .?'

'David, Sister. David Smithson.'

'Well, how can I help, David?'

'Do you think you could get Dr Devine in here? He's really the person I want to speak to but I didn't know how to get him on his own.'

She was more and more intrigued. 'I'll put the coffee on while you have your little chat.'

She put her head round the door. 'Dr Devine, could you spare me a minute?'

Carl looked up from the charts and smiled. 'Of course.'

'I was going to come in to see you,' he began as he closed the door behind him. He looked across at the young man in surprise, clearly not expecting him to be there.

'This is David Smithson, Carl. He's got some more questions for you, I believe.'

She was boiling the kettle, spooning coffee into the cafetière and putting cups and saucers on a tray. Turning round, she saw that the two men were simply standing in the middle of the floor, staring at each other.

She hesitated. 'Is something the matter?'

The young man had turned quite white. She watched him look across at Carl, as if sizing him up.

'I think you may be. . .' David Smithson began hesitantly. 'In fact, I'm sure you're my father.'

Jenni sank down onto the nearest chair, her hands automatically raised to her mouth as if to prevent herself from crying out. This was all too incredible! This eighteen-year-old boy couldn't possibly be Carl's son. . .or could he. . .?

This time she saw the blood drain from Carl's face.

She held her breath as she saw him opening his mouth to speak.

'David,' he whispered hoarsely, 'David. Is it really you?'

And then Carl moved forward to put his arms around the young man, holding him in a bear hug. For several seconds Jenni witnessed the profoundly moving scene. She could feel tears, prickling at the back of her eyes.

When the two men separated she could see that their eyes were moist. The hows and the wherefores would be explained in due course, she was sure—not least how Carl, at the age of thirty-six, could be the father of this eighteen-year-old boy whose name was Smithson.

Looking at the two of them, she had no doubt now that David had got to be Carl's son. The dead give-away was the hair! She was relieved to know that it wasn't her own obsession with Carl that had made the connection earlier.

'Coffee?' She put the cups down on small tables beside the chairs where Carl and David were now sprawled. Two sets of dark eyes looked up at her, Carl's registering astonishment and David's relief.

'Would you like me to leave you two alone?' Jenni asked gently.

'No, please stay, Jenni,' Carl said quickly. 'I didn't tell you I had a son, did I?'

'No, you didn't.' She sat down near her desk and took a sip of coffee. 'How long is it since you two saw each other?'

Carl cleared his throat. 'I haven't seen David since he was six months old.'

Jenni put down her cup and saucer. 'So. . .?'

'David, where have you sprung from today?' Carl asked quietly.

'Originally I'd got myself a medical school place in the States for this September. Then Mum. . .'

'How is your mum?' Carl interrupted.

'Oh, you know Mum. . .I expect.' David paused awkwardly. 'She's fine. Anyway, she's decided to leave her current husband because she's found a new boyfriend. I decided it was time to find my real dad—I didn't want to wait another six years while I did my medical training.'

He leaned back in his chair, his eyes fixed on Carl. 'Mum had told me you were a doctor in England so I contacted the British Medical Association. They told me you were going to be senior registrar at Moortown General, starting in April. So I persuaded the powers-that-be to get me a transfer. . .and here I am.'

'And you'll be here for the next six years,' Jenni said, almost to herself, as she looked across at Carl, wondering how he would take this.

He certainly seemed overjoyed to see his son, but this new turn of events would certainly upset his plans. How about his prestigious appointment with the cruise line in November? His son had sought him out only months before he was planning to move on again.

So what had happened to David in the intervening years between the age of six months and eighteen years? And who was his mother?

'Sister.' Staff Nurse Carol Thomas poked her head round the door. 'Mrs Derby's drip needs changing and she's asking if you'll do it. Sorry, I didn't mean to interrupt but. . .'

'That's OK, Carol. I was just coming out to get on with some work.'

Jenni stood up, feeling relieved to escape the tension.

It was a joyous reunion but it was obviously going to pose more problems than it solved.

'Jenni, I'd like to see you this evening,' Carl said quickly as she made for the door. 'Will you be at the cottage?'

She hesitated. She could phone him with her news and then she wouldn't have to see him alone again. But she could see that his initial euphoria at seeing his son was turning into apprehension as he began to grasp his responsibilities.

He was obviously out of his depth as he struggled to come to terms with his emotions. Surely he would want to be with his son on the first evening, wouldn't he?

'I'll be home soon after eight,' she said, glancing at David who was pretending not to listen in. 'Would you like to come too, David?'

The look of gratitude on the young man's face gave her a warm glow. She'd invited him because she felt sorry that he'd come all this way and didn't realise that he would only have a few months with his father. And also there would be safety in numbers! With David to chaperone them there was no danger that she would be carried away by her feelings for Carl.

'That would be super. Thanks a lot, Sister.'

'The name's Jenni.'

Carl flashed her a grateful smile. 'If it would help I could pick up a take-away, Jenni.'

'That's OK. I'll get something out of the freezer. There's some Bolognese sauce. I could cook some spaghetti to go with it.'

'Great!' David said. 'Did you make the sauce yourself?'

'Of course.' What was so unusual about that? Maybe this was a boy who'd never experienced home cooking.

'I do a batch bake every few weeks. Look, I'd better go. I'll see you both tonight.'

For the rest of the day Jenni's mind kept flitting from her medical duties to the unknown saga of Carl's son. How much would they tell her about his mother, the woman who was going off with her new boyfriend? And where had David acquired the name Smithson?

As the questions forced themselves upon her she realised that she'd almost forgotten that she had to tell Carl her news. She had to decide whether to go ahead with another conception operation or make an appointment at the Bramdale clinic.

As soon as she'd handed over to Sister Maggie Warren she headed for Cragdale. Summer had finally arrived in the valley. In fact, there had been a positive heat wave during the past week. The carnations she'd arranged in the fireplace several days ago were wilting. She hurried outside into the garden and replaced them with roses and ferns.

No time to dust! In the kitchen she put the Bolognese sauce in the microwave before setting a pan of salted water on the stove.

Did she have time for a shower? She always felt so dirty after a day in hospital. Yes, if she was quick.

Tyres squealed on the drive as she ran back down the stairs, feeling refreshed in her clean cotton skirt and T-shirt.

Opening the door, she was surprised to see two cars in her narrow drive, one behind the other. Carl led the way in his sleek two-seater sports car and David followed on behind in what could only be described as an old banger.

'Quite a contrast in vehicles!' Jenni said as she watched the two men climbing out.

David grinned. 'I bought it yesterday at a car auction. Dad thinks it's a heap of junk. I don't care, so long as it gets me from A to B.'

'It's the safety element I'm worried about,' Carl said, looking across affectionately at his son.

Jenni felt a lump in her throat as she watched them. They were already close. She wondered if Carl had dared to tell David that he was going to leave Moortwon in the autumn.

'Come in, supper's nearly ready.'

They followed her into the kitchen and leaned against the sink as she put the spaghetti into the boiling water.

'Would you like me to set the table, Jenni?' David asked. 'I always used to help my mum at home so I'm fully house-trained.'

'Thanks, David. Cutlery and table mats in this drawer.'

She continued to lower the spaghetti into the pan. 'Where's home?'

David laughed. 'Good question! Most recently it was in Detroit, but Mum's gone to New Zealand so. . .'

He gave a resigned shrug. 'I'm going to make England my home now. I mean, that's where I was born, wasn't it, Dad?'

'It certainly was. You were born in the London hospital where I, subsequently, went on to do my medical training.'

Carl paused, glancing around the kitchen. 'Where do you keep your corkscrew, Jenni?'

'It's hanging on the wall in that rack.'

She put the lid on the saucepan and turned round to watch Carl open the raffia-encased bottle of red wine he'd brought with him.

'I thought *madame* would like Italian wine to complement her spaghetti Bolognese this evening,' Carl said, drawing the cork out of the Chianti bottle.

'I'd better not drink any alcohol,' David said. 'I've arranged to take some friends to the Coach and Horses after supper and I'm the designated driver.'

'So what can I get you?' Jenni said, opening the fridge. 'Coca-Cola, orange juice. . .?'

'Milk, please,' David said, spotting the large carton. Jenni smiled. 'Help yourself.'

The three of them sat at the kitchen table, Carl and Jenni sipping wine and David with his glass of milk.

'Where are you staying, David?' Jenni asked.

'I'm renting a bedsit near the hospital for the summer. I've only taken it on a weekly basis because it's not very salubrious. In fact it's a dump!' David gave a cheerful grin. 'When I find something better I'll move.'

Jenni stood up to test the texture of the spaghetti. It was almost ready. She waited by the stove.

'So, what do you intend to do until your medical studies start in September?'

The young man smiled happily. 'I've been dead lucky. I applied for a job as a hospital porter and they told me yesterday that I can start next week. That was when I went out and bought the car. I've worked out that my wages will pay for the running of the car, my rent and still leave me something for food and the odd glass of milk.'

Carl smiled. 'The optimism of youth! You'd better let me help you out, David. Old cars sometimes break down and. . .'

'It's OK, Dad,' David said firmly. 'I can manage.'

Jenni saw the flash of defiance in the young man's eyes. Did he resent having grown up without his natural father? Was he anxious to make it clear that he wanted to be independent of Carl, even though he'd gone to enormous lengths to search him out?

As she drained the spaghetti over the sink she realised that this relationship between father and son was not going to be all plain sailing. Adjustments were going to have to be made on both sides.

'This is the best spaghetti Bolognese I've ever tasted!' David said, as he quickly demolished the food Jenni had put on his plate.

'And that's high praise indeed from someone with an Italian great-grandmother!' Carl said.

David looked surprised. 'I didn't know my great-grandmother was Italian.'

'We've got a lot of catching up to do, son,' Carl said, his voice husky.

'Another helping, David?' Jenni asked, as she watched Carl take a handkerchief from his pocket and blow his nose vigorously.

'Yes, please!'

David pushed back his chair at the end of the meal. 'I hope you don't think me impolite, but I really have to run now. I've promised to pick up these friends and. . .'

'That's quite all right, David,' Jenni said. 'We understand, don't we, Carl?'

Carl smiled. 'I was young myself—many years ago. Drive carefully!'

He followed his son to the front door. 'You'd better let me direct you out into the road. This is an impossible driveway.'

'Thanks very much!' Jenni said as she walked out into the garden.

'Why don't you make it semicircular, Jenni?' David

said. 'If you removed part of that wall and enlarged the sides of. . .'

'That's what I intend to do when I get around to finding the right builders or whoever it is I need for a job like that.'

'No problem!' David said. 'I've worked on a building site during my summer vacations. I'll come over and do it for you when I'm not working at the hospital.'

'Oh, I couldn't possibly. . .'

'Please let me, Jenni. I'd really enjoy it!'

She hesitated. Such enthusiasm was overwhelming! 'Thanks, David.'

Carl was smiling when he returned from waving David out into the road. 'So, how do you like my son, Jenni?'

'I think he's charming.' She hesitated. 'I don't want to pry but I'd love to know why you haven't seen each other for eighteen years.'

His carefree expression clouded over. 'It's a long story.'

'I'm not going anywhere,' she said quietly. 'But only if you really want to tell me.'

'I do.'

'I'll bring the coffee out here and we can sit under the stars,' she said, indicating the worn iron seat in front of the ivy-covered wall of the house.

Returning from the kitchen, she set the tray down on the ancient wrought-iron table, dusting away a few leaves with her fingers. The light from the sitting-room window shone on them, adding to the weak glow from the new moon.

Carl turned to look at Jenni. 'This is terribly romantic, sitting here in the moonlight, don't you think?'

'Absolutely!' She recognised his bantering tone.

Today had been a day full of strong emotions for Carl and he was unsure how to cope with them.

She waited. He took a sip of his coffee before he returned the cup to the table and leant back against the seat, stretching his arms up and placing his hands behind his neck.

'I really don't know where to begin.'

'Tell me about David's mother,' she said quietly.

Strangely enough, that was the first thing she wanted to find out about. She was longing to know if Carl had loved David's mother and, if so, why they'd split up.

'I told you about being brought up by my Italian grandmother in east London, didn't I? Well, Grandma died when I was sixteen. I managed to stay on in her flat. The rent was always a problem, but I did a paper round and worked in a Saturday job so I scraped by. Then Samantha came on the scene.'

He stretched out his hands in front of him, carefully pointing the tips of his fingers together as he conjured up the past.

'Samantha was David's mother?'

He nodded. 'She was in my class at the local comprehensive. She lived in a children's home because she was an orphan. We were both sixteen when we started going out together. She used to come to the flat and very soon we became lovers.'

He cleared his throat. 'She told me she was on the Pill. I think she probably was, but she was such a scatterbrain that she probably forgot to take it. Anyway, she was very quickly pregnant and begging me to marry her. Looking back, I think she was desperate to have her own home.'

He took a deep breath. 'I was seventeen when we got married. I carried on going to school so I could get enough qualifications to get into medical school. Soon after my eighteenth birthday baby David was born.'

Jenni heard the deep sigh as he paused to take another breath.

'How did you feel about being a father when you were so young?'

'I adored the baby! But I quickly found that I couldn't stand Samantha. And the feeling became mutual. She used to nag me about money, beg me to give up the idea of going to medical school and get myself a job. But I wasn't going to throw away my ambition. I told her that one day she would thank me for keeping on course, but Samantha was only ever able to live for the moment.'

For a few seconds he looked up at the sky, as if to draw inspiration from the twinkling stars. There was absolutely no sound—it was as if the whole valley was asleep.

'I got my place at St Celine's Hospital in London. When I got home after my first day there the flat was empty. There was a note from Samantha, telling me that she'd gone away with someone who could give her a better home than I could.'

Jenni drew in her breath as she heard the deep sadness in Carl's voice. 'And the baby?'

'She'd taken David with her.' Carl's voice was now decidedly shaky. 'That was the bit I couldn't take. I went mad, searching for her. It was a neighbour, an old friend of my Gran's, who told me what had happened.'

Jenni's heart went out to Carl as she waited for him to regain his composure.

'Apparently, Samantha had been in the habit of leaving baby David with this neighbour and going out to the pub at lunchtimes when I wasn't there. She'd met a tourist from South Africa.

'Old enough to be her father but filthy rich, was how my neighbour described him. He'd often driven Samantha back to the flat in his expensive car and she used to invite him in.'

'So you never saw her again?'

'I couldn't afford to follow her to South Africa. I'd just started my medical studies. I had to keep going. But I vowed I would go and find my son as soon as I qualified.'

'And did you?'

'The year before I graduated I got a letter from a firm of solicitors in Johannesburg, enclosing divorce papers. I signed everything and made a note of Samantha's address. As soon as I graduated I scraped together the fare and flew out to Johannesburg. When I got to the house she'd gone.'

'Where?'

'John Smithson, the man she'd lived with, said he had no idea where she was and I believed him. I actually felt quite sorry for him. He said he'd loved David as if he'd been his own son and now he was devastated. Samantha had gone off to America with a rich business-man and taken David with her.'

'I flew back to London, and it was at that point that I decided to harden my heart and abandon the search. I simply put all my feelings and emotions on ice. But I couldn't settle in hospital work. I wanted to continue to practise medicine but I had to keep moving on. When I took my first post as a ship's doctor I found it helped to be out at sea. Always going somewhere. . .'

Jenni heard his voice trail away. 'But you went back to hospital in London for a while, didn't you?'

He nodded. 'Soon after I turned thirty I thought I'd better establish myself as a serious doctor. I went back to London and worked as a junior registrar and then as a senior registrar in obstetrics and gynaecology. But, as I told you, the itchy feet returned and I'll be on the high seas again in November.'

'Have you told David?'

He hesitated. 'No, I haven't.'

'He'll have to know sooner or later.'

'He's a big boy! Sorry, Jenni, I didn't mean to snap at you.'

'That's OK. I understand.' she said quietly. 'It's been quite a day.'

She paused. 'There's something I have to tell you. I. . .I've started my period.'

In the half-light she couldn't make out the expression in his eyes.

'We'll have to try again,' he said quietly. 'That won't be a problem for you, will it?'

'No. . .no, of course not!'

There, she'd committed herself! It would be pointless to consider AI treatment. Somehow she would put her feelings on hold when they next got together. She would be stronger this time, now that she knew how easy it was to get carried away when she was in Carl's arms. . .

He was leaning towards her. She held her breath because now she could distinguish the look of exquisite tenderness in his eyes. Oh, she could drown in those dark brown liquid pools! Deep down inside she felt a warm stirring of emotion and something akin to passion.

She tried to turn away but he had taken hold of her shoulders, and his face. . .his lips were, oh, so close.

One part of her was praying that he wouldn't kiss

her, while the other was longing for the feel of his
sensuous lips.

'You've been such a help, Jenni,' he was saying. 'I
don't know what I would have done without you.'

And then he kissed her, and she forgot how hard she
was trying to keep her emotions in check. His lips were
warm, moist and infinitely disturbing. She could feel her
response to his kiss quivering through her entire body.

She pulled away, running a hand through her hair and
taking a deep breath in the hope of an instant recovery.

'Well, I'm glad I was able to help,' she said quickly.

She saw that he was smiling—his twinkling eyes
gave him away. He'd felt her response and he wasn't
fooled in the least by her futile attempt to ignore the
electric sparks flashing between them.

'Shall we set a date?' he said in a deliberately matter
of fact tone.

'A date?'

'For our next conception operation. Let's see. . .' He
was pulling out his diary.

'In a couple of weeks,' Jenni said. 'That brings us
to the middle of July. How about the fifteenth?'

'The fifteenth it is.' He stood up. 'Better get back.'

She followed him over to his car. 'It's very kind of
David to offer to do my drive, but I don't want to take
up all his free time.'

'Nonsense! He'll enjoy it. I'll give him a hand myself
when I'm free.'

'I couldn't possibly. . .'

'Silence, woman! You're outvoted. I worked as a
labourer in my vacations too. Used to be a dab hand
with a pneumatic drill.'

He gave her a quick peck on the cheek and climbed

into the car. She went out into the road to help him reverse.

Going back inside, the house felt strangely empty. She'd always enjoyed closing the front door and entering her own little independent territory but tonight something was missing.

She turned out the downstairs lights and climbed the stairs. She covered herself with a sheet. It was much too hot for the duvet. The duvet under which she'd made love with Carl. . .

It wasn't making love! she told herself. We were trying to conceive my baby. That's all it was. . .and that's all it must be the next time.

CHAPTER SIX

JENNI pulled off the page from her office calendar. July fifteenth. It was here at last! Tonight she and Carl would have another attempt at conceiving a baby. For days she'd been unable to put it out of her mind.

She sat down at her desk and started to check through the input and output charts of her post-operative patients. Yes, the night staff had done a good job. They'd filled in all the details she'd asked for.

She planned to go round and see all these patients. . .in a little while. . .when she'd had a minute to clear her head of all the personal trivia floating around up there.

She looked over to the open window. The hot sun was beating down on the hospital roof. Her hands felt sticky already. A busy day lay ahead of her and then. . .hardly a relaxing evening!

But as she remembered the last time she'd gone to bed with Carl she gave a shiver of excited anticipation. She'd never felt like this about anybody before.

She'd seen him every day for the past two weeks. David had made a start on her drive and was doing a brilliant job. Carl had also been out to the cottage to help. Last weekend she'd had these two strong, stripped-to-the-waist men working for hours in her garden. As she'd dispensed drinks and food she'd suddenly realised that she was becoming just like her sister, Gemma, her two sisters-in-law and her mother.

She was allowing the men to take over! It was Carl

who'd insisted that he and David would construct the drive for her. She remembered how she'd had reservations about it when it had been suggested. She would have preferred to call in the professionals, pay the bill and have done with it. She'd never liked to accept favours from people.

But Carl had said, 'Quiet, woman! You're outvoted!'

The amazing thing was that she didn't resent this! She'd loved every minute when she'd fetched and carried for Carl and his son last Sunday. Whatever was happening to her independent spirit?

The door opened. 'Anne Fields has been in the birthing pool for an hour, Sister,' said Carol Thomas. 'You asked me to inform you when we thought we were getting close to the birth.'

Jenni jumped up from her desk. 'I'm coming.'

The birthing pool was a new addition to the obstetrics unit and there had been some controversy when it was first introduced. But it had proved highly successful and popular with the patients who'd requested it. However, she still made a point of being on hand for as many births as possible.

She hurried down the ward into the prenatal unit. Her patient was leaning back in the water and her husband was rubbing her back and making soothing noises. Margaret Peel, the staff midwife, was checking the temperature of the water.

Gently Jenni eased her patient onto her side so that she could ascertain how far the birth canal was dilated. She checked the foetal heartbeat with a Pinard's stethoscope. The baby was giving off healthy sounds.

'Won't be long now, Anne,' she said in a reassuring voice.

Anne Fields closed her eyes as she floated in the pool.

'It's so relaxing in the water. Oh, hang on, there's another contraction coming, Sister. . .'

'Deep breaths now, Anne,' Jenni said, kneeling down to hold her patient's shoulders, massaging away the tension from the back of her neck.

The baby's head was appearing. 'Pant now, Anne,' Jenni said.

Staff Nurse Peel had taken hold of the baby's head and was easing the shoulders down through the birth canal. The rest of the body flopped out into the water. Jenni reached forward to take the baby from her staff nurse. Quickly she tied off and cut the cord, before handing the baby to his mother.

'A boy!' Anne Fields said, her eyes glowing with happiness.

The young father kissed his wife. 'You were so brave,' he said.

Anne smiled. 'I think floating in the water helped, Jim. What do you think, Sister?'

'For some mothers it's excellent, and you're obviously one of those.'

'Shall I book the pool for our next baby?' Jim said with a wide grin.

His wife pulled a face. 'The birthing pool helped, but you can have the next one.'

Jenni took the baby from his mother and began the routine postnatal checks. She loved the distinctive smell on his newborn skin. His dear little hands waved in front of him as if he was testing out his new environment.

'What a treasure you are,' she said as she weighed him. 'Three and a half kilos. That's fine!'

Looking up, she saw with a start that Carl had come into the birthing pool area and was watching her with a fond expression.

'Isn't he gorgeous?' she said. 'Just look at those perfect little hands!'

The midwives were looking at her. She suddenly realised that she was being totally unprofessional. Obstetric sisters usually got on with the job and didn't get over-excited about it. Babies were delivered every hour of the day, and the routine usually dulled their emotional response.

But Jenni knew that she was different. She wanted her own baby more than anything else in the world! She looked at Carl and her heart gave a little hop, skip and a jump of delicious anticipation.

His expression changed to one of complete pro-fessionalism.

'I came to tell you we've got an emergency patient— just arrived on the ward.'

Jenni handed the baby to Staff Nurse Peel. 'You'd better finish off the routine checks, Margaret. Give me a report when you've finished, please.'

She followed Carl out of the door. 'What kind of emergency?'

'Pete Jones is examining the patient now. She's got a high temperature, intense abdominal pain, rapid pulse. . .'

'Could be any number of things,' Jenni said as she went into the new patient's cubicle.

Dr Jones, their junior registrar, looked up in relief as Carl and Jenni arrived.

'She seems to have a lot of pain just here,' he said, placing his hands over the lower part of the patient's abdomen.

'Let me have a look,' Carl said, leaning over the bed, after a quick glance at the case notes.

'Hello, Fay, how long have you been feeling poorly?'

The patient tried to raise herself up on her elbow but fell back against the pillows. Jenni could see the care-worn expression on her lined face. The case notes said that she was forty-five. She looked older. Her grey hair spread out across the pillow and her thin arms twitched nervously at the sheet.

'Haven't been feeling myself for a few days now, Doctor. Not since I had my period last week. It was an absolute shocker. Never had one like that before. I had to go to bed it was that bad.'

'How was the period before that, Fay?' Jenni asked gently.

'Let me see—can't actually remember. That one was months ago. I must be in the change.'

'Try and think how many months ago, Fay,' Carl said, sitting down on the edge of the patient's bed and taking hold of her hot, shaking hand.

'I think it was around Easter. . . Yes, it was the week before Easter because. . .'

Fay Procter continued to reminisce about what had happened the week before Easter while Carl, Jenni and Pete quietly discussed the case at the far end of the bed.

'It could be an incomplete miscarriage,' Carl said.

'That's what I was thinking,' Jenni said.

Carl went back to their patient's side and took hold of her hand again. 'When you missed those periods did it ever occur to you that you might be pregnant, Fay?'

'Of course not! I'm too old! I'm in the change, Doctor. Jack and I haven't bothered taking any pre-cautions since I turned forty. Didn't need to, did we?'

'Well, I'm not sure, Fay,' Carl said diplomatically. 'There's a possibility that the period you had last week may have been a miscarriage.'

'Well, why do I feel so bad if it's all over and done with, Doctor?'

The patient was running her hands distractedly through her hair and breathing rapidly.

'Shall I call Theatre, Carl?' Jenni whispered.

He nodded. 'Fay, I'm going to give you something to make you drowsy, then I'll take you down to Theatre. You'll go off to sleep and I can check out if anything's been left in your womb. Once we can be sure that nothing's been left inside you'll start to improve.'

Jenni returned, carrying a kidney dish which contained a hypodermic syringe and the pre-operative drug.

'They're all ready for you in Theatre,' she said, as Carl injected their patient.

Jenni looked up and smiled at the young hospital porter who'd arrived with the theatre trolley.

'You'll be quite safe with David,' Carl told Fay. 'But, just to make sure, I'll walk along to Theatre with you. Here, let me give you a hand, young man. . .'

Father and son helped Jenni to ease Fay Procter onto the trolley. The patient looked up drowsily, her eyes studying the faces of the two men.

'Must be the drugs, but I could swear I'm seeing double,' she said, before drifting off to sleep.

Jenni looked across the patient towards Carl and David. 'I'm not the only one who thinks you look like twins—separated by eighteen years, of course.'

David grinned. 'Maybe I could do your job, Dad, and you could do mine.'

'Serve your time first, my boy,' Carl said affectionately, as he helped David manoeuvre the trolley out through the cubicle.

Jenni walked with them as far as the nurses' station and watched as they went out through the swing doors.

'Just can't believe that's the divine Carl's son,' Staff Nurse Penny Drew said, flicking a hand over the blonde hair that had escaped from her cap. 'They look more like brothers. Dr Devine must have been very young when David was born.'

'Must have been,' Jenni said evenly. 'Have you finished the dressings, Penny?'

'Almost,' Penny said, making her way hurriedly to the treatment-room.

Jenni went off down the ward towards the obstetrics unit. She wanted to check on the newly delivered baby boy. As she went in through the swing doors she was thinking about the way the grapevine had hummed for the past two weeks since David Smithson's arrival. He still maintained the surname that his mother's first boy-friend had given him.

Carl had explained to Jenni that Smithson was the name on David's passport and all his medical school papers. But as soon as they could sort out the legal situation with Carl's solicitor David's surname was going to revert to Devine.

Carl had made no secret of the situation. He'd proudly told everyone that David was his son. What he hadn't mentioned was anything about David's mother. Jenni had been quizzed about this but had refused to divulge any details.

The new baby was suckling at his mother's breast. Jenni checked that the details of the birth had been written up, before going on to her next prenatal patient.

Theresa Jordan, in her late thirties, was making very slow progress and getting tired of waiting.

'I thought I would have had the baby by now, Sister,' she said, leaning back on her pillows. 'How far on am I?'

Jenni checked the birth canal. 'You've got a long way to go, Theresa. Get up and have a walk around the ward. That might get things moving.'

Her patient pulled a wry face. 'There have been two women who came in after me and they've already had their babies.'

'I know—the queueing system doesn't work with babies. They've got minds of their own and like to decide exactly when they're going to put in an appearance,' Jenni said gently. 'I'm afraid you'll just have to be patient.'

'But couldn't you induce me or something?' Tessa said.

'That's not necessary in your case,' Jenni said. 'I'll keep popping back to see how you're getting on.'

Simon Delaware arrived in the unit, asking Jenni to do a round of all his patients with him. When the round was finished Jenni had to catch up on her own routine work.

Post-operative patients arrived back from Theatre throughout the day and had to be carefully monitored. At the end of the afternoon David, accompanied by Carl, wheeled in their last patient, Fay Procter.

Jenni supervised Fay's transition back into bed.

'We kept Fay in Recovery for a while because she took a long time to come round,' Carl said.

'Was it what we suspected?' Jenni asked as she checked the IV cannula in Fay's arm, before regulating the flow of intravenous blood.

Carl nodded. 'Yes, it was an incomplete miscarriage. I cleaned out the remains of the pregnancy so we've got rid of the source of infection. Fay's on antibiotics and her high temperature is returning to normal. Pulse still too fast. Get one of your conscientious nurses to special her.'

'I'll do it myself for a while. They're all busy at the moment,' Jenni said.

David pushed the trolley out of the cubicle.

'You're not going to be late off duty, are you?' Carl asked.

She felt the colour rushing to her cheeks. 'I'll try not to be.'

'Would you like to come over to my place? David's changing his duty shifts this evening. He's going off duty now, to return at eight for the night shift, so we'll be quite alone. I'll cook you supper.'

Jenni smiled. 'You're on!'

She turned her attention back to Fay, who was drows-ily beginning to ask questions about the outcome of her operation. She reassured her patient that she was well on the road to recovery, before removing Fay's theatre gown, sponging her hands and face, combing her hair and putting her into a clean nightdress.

Staff Midwife Margaret Peel poked her head into the cubicle. 'Theresa Jordan's baby's arrived, Sister!'

'Thank goodness for that! Everything OK?'

'Perfect! A little girl—three kilos—Theresa's over the moon. It all happened very quickly once she'd got through the first stage.'

'I thought it might,' Jenni said. 'Give Theresa my congratulations and tell her I'll be along as soon as I can make it.'

Jenni was relieved to hand over the Nightingale reins to Maggie Warren at eight o'clock. Her feet were aching and she needed a shower. When Carl had suggested that she go to his place it had seemed like a good idea. That had been because she was curious to see the house he'd just moved into, and also it would mean that she didn't have to cook the supper.

She stood in the shower cubicle in the women staff's changing-room and let the water cascade over her body. Mmm, that felt good! It certainly helped the transition between professional woman and willing concubine!

She stepped out of the shower and slipped into the clean jeans and shirt she'd brought with her that morning. She told herself to get into a casual mood—a relaxed attitude was essential.

Driving away from the hospital, she realised that she wasn't sure where Carl's newly acquired house was. A week ago he'd told her that he and David had moved into a rented house in Cragdale—on the other side of the valley from her cottage.

She'd gathered that Carl had been to look at David's flat and had considered it unfit to live in! This had spurred him on to find a place for the two of them.

Carl had told her that he'd convinced David that he'd planned to get himself a house and that the place he'd found was too big for one person. He needed the pitter-patter of enormous shoes to stop him from feeling lonely!

Jenni drove down into Cragdale village, telling herself that she should have paid more attention when Carl was giving her directions. Left at the pub, over the bridge, on a bit, climb the hill, halfway up. . .

There it was! The White House—painted a brilliant white by the people who Carl had said were desperate to rent out while they went around the world on their wedding anniversary cruise of a lifetime. Even the wooden shutters were painted white.

Apparently, the couple had been forced to set off before the house had been let, and the estate agent's instructions had been to take a lower rent from anyone who could move in immediately.

As she drove in through wrought-iron gates she glanced at the dormer windows on the first floor. They were open wide to the summer evening and she could just distinguish flowered chintz curtains, peeping out. She felt her pulse rate increasing. Was that Carl's bedroom? Was that where. . .?

'Jenni!'

Carl had come out onto the wide stone steps that led into the house and was standing there, looking relaxed, casual and impossibly desirable in off-white cotton trousers and a white polo shirt, open at the neck.

She would have no problem relaxing with him this evening! The problem would be in pretending that she was totally unaffected by the proceedings.

'I thought I might have to send out a search party,' Carl said, coming down the steps to meet her.

'Your instructions were good.'

She shielded her eyes from the glow of the setting sun as she looked across the valley.

'Look, you can just see my cottage—to the right of those trees.'

He put a hand casually on her shoulders. 'I know. We'll be able to send semaphore messages to each other.'

'And save our phone bills,' she said, desperately aware of the hand on her shoulder. 'Well, are you going to show me the inside of this palatial dwelling?'

He led the way up the steps. 'It is rather grand, isn't it? I've been terribly lucky to get it for the rent I'm paying. It comes complete with daily cleaning woman and resident cat.'

As if on cue, a black and white cat strolled along the

hall carpet to meet them. Jenni bent down to stroke her
and she began to purr.

'Mopsy likes you,' Carl said, opening a solid oak
door leading from the hall. 'This is the drawing-room.'

'Oh, very grand!'

Jenni looked round the large room, admiring the deep
red velvet curtains in the wide bay window, the Chinese
carpet complete with dragons in the middle of the
polished oak floor and the vast collection of antique
furniture.

'Don't know how they could bear to rent it out to
strangers,' Jenni said.

'Maureen, the cleaning lady, who loves to chat, told
me that Mr and Mrs Crossley are retired and they
couldn't afford their cruise unless they subsidised it by
letting out the house. Come and see the kitchen.'

'It's huge!' Jenni said, making a bee-line for the
rocking chair by the side of the open range. She sat
down, and began rocking backwards and forwards.

'Oh, this is lovely. My grandma had a rocking chair
like this.'

Carl grinned. 'Mine didn't. Are you ready for your
pre-med?'

She smiled. 'Of course. What's been written up on
my chart, Doctor?'

'I'll get the prescribed dose,' he said as the cork
popped out of the champagne bottle.

He brought her glass over to the rocking chair. They
clinked glasses together.

She took a sip. 'Hope we're successful this time.'

'I'm sure we will be,' he said, 'whatever the
outcome.'

She was left to figure out Carl's cryptic remark as
he turned away and went over to the oven. Was he

beginning to enjoy their conception operations as much
as she was? Were they both trying too hard at their
make-believe situation?

'When I said I'd cook what I meant was that I'd
reheat a Marks and Spencer's special,' he said, his back
still turned towards her. 'So I hope I haven't got you
here under false pretences.'

'It smells delicious. What is it?'

'*Lasagne verde*. The Italian influence again.'

'Where do you keep your knives and forks?' she said,
putting her champagne glass on the kitchen table. 'I
presume we're not going through into the baronial
dining-hall I glimpsed through there.'

He grinned. 'Dead right, we're not! It's more cosy
in here.'

She set the knives and forks on either side of the
long kitchen table. Carl served the lasagne onto blue
and white willow pattern plates, before placing a large
wooden salad bowl between them. Jenni picked up the
wooden servers and tossed the salad in the vinaigrette
dressing that Carl had prepared.

'This is good,' she said, looking across the table
at Carl.

'Yes, isn't it?'

She saw the tender expression in his eyes, and bent
her head to put more lasagne on her fork.

He produced strawberries and cream to follow the
lasagne.

'You're spoiling me,' she said.

'Trying to.'

She heard the huskiness in his voice and felt the
steady mounting of suspense deep down inside her.

'Would you like coffee now. . .or afterwards?' he
asked in a matter-of-fact tone.

She hesitated. 'Maybe after the operation, Doctor,' she said, in what was an attempt to revert to their make-believe game. Looking at the enigmatic expression in Carl's eyes, she wondered if he was becoming tired of the pretence.

He smiled. 'In that case, let me show you the way to the master bedroom. I think you'll like it.'

She was prepared to love it even before she'd seen it, and the reality didn't disappoint her. Chintz curtains hung at the open dormer windows, through which she could faintly smell the scent of the roses down in the garden. The wide king-size bed with the sheet turned back looked infinitely inviting.

She kicked off her shoes and padded over the thick white carpet. 'May I use the bathroom first, Carl?'

'Would you believe there's a His and Hers! You're going in the right direction for *madame's* little room— mine's across the landing.'

She was tempted to run herself a bath in the enormous, antique porcelain contraption, complete with brass taps and clawed feet. But she settled for a few seconds in the shower and a dab of scent behind the ears. From the depths of her capacious shoulder-bag she pulled out the flimsy, rose-pink chiffon robe she'd bought last week.

In the Moortown boutique she'd succeeded in convincing herself that she badly needed a new robe. It had nothing to do with Carl!

He was waiting in the bed when she emerged from the bathroom. He whistled softly under his breath.

'Wow! You look nice. Is that new?'

'What? This old thing?'

They both laughed.

'Come over here,' he said, his voice gravelly.

She crossed over to the bed, her bare feet revelling in the lush pile of the carpet and her whole body awakening in anticipation. He pulled back the sheet. She climbed in. He took her face in his hands and kissed her, oh, so gently, on the lips.

She shivered ever so slightly.

'It's OK, Jenni, I'm not going to hurt you,' he said gently.

'I know that. That's not... Look, Carl, I'm finding being close to you like this is so difficult. I don't know how to explain but...'

'Jenni, I know what you're trying to tell me and I understand. Believe me, I'm having the same problem...probably more than you.'

He gave a nervous laugh. 'It just proves that we're only human. From a medical point of view, close contact with each other is bound to trigger off our erogenous zones. But there's absolutely no reason why we shouldn't enjoy being together.'

His hands had begun to caress her breasts. Sensual shivers were running down her skin.

'But it won't change what we agreed on,' he whispered. 'It's your baby we're trying to conceive. I'll keep my promise not to interfere with your future plans.'

She felt a pang of disappointment at his words and realised that she would have preferred him to say that he wanted to share her life. In spite of all her resolutions and all the problems it would pose, she'd been unable to prevent herself from falling in love with him.

She closed her eyes as she gave in to the sensual waves of passion that were washing over her. She was floating on cloud nine, living for the moment—giving out all the love she could. She revelled in the exquisite fusion of their bodies and when the anticipated climax arrived she clung to him, wanting the moment to last for ever.

He stroked her hair. 'Jenni, are you OK?'

She lay very still, unwilling to return to the banality of their make-believe situation.

'I'm fine,' she whispered, her eyes moist as she hid them against his shoulder.

'Hey, you're not crying, are you?'

He raised his head to look down at her.

'Don't be silly!'

She pulled herself away, grabbed a tissue from the bedside table and blew her nose vigorously.

He was watching her, his eyes tenderly affectionate.

'Don't go,' he said quietly. 'Stay here and lie still. Doctor's orders. Give the poor sperm a chance.'

She went back into the circle of his arms, telling herself that they were back on course. The love-making was over. This was the post-operative period. Time to analyse the situation.

'I hope I've conceived this time,' she said, in what was meant to be a bright, professional voice.

'I hope so too, but a repeat operation would be no problem.'

She remained silent, wondering how on earth she would ever get through a repeat performance without completely losing her heart to him.

CHAPTER SEVEN

JENNI had given herself a split duty next day. After her morning's work on Nightingale the whole of the afternoon stretched out in front of her. She could go home to the cottage or. . .

She felt an overwhelming desire to go over to see her mother. She wanted the reassurance that nothing had changed—that normal life was carrying on around her—even though she was feeling shell-shocked after her evening with Carl.

As she drove over the moorland road towards Riversdale she told herself that she was still in control of her life. She still held the reins on Nightingale; she was still mistress of her own house.

Carl would soon be leaving Moortown so she wouldn't have to worry about the fact that she'd fallen in love. Although the feeling was excitingly, deliciously, out of this world she felt as if she were falling apart at the seams! But she reasoned that if Carl wasn't around her she would start to feel normal again.

A sheep ran across in front of the car and she braked hard, stalling the engine.

Who am I kidding? she thought as she restarted the car. She knew she would be heartbroken when he went away. But she'd survive. This was a temporary aberration she was suffering from. She would cope without him. She'd regain her calm, uncomplicated sense of independence, and when the baby came. . .

When the baby came it would be even worse, she

116

realised. It would be sure to have dark hair, with a hint of gold; it would grow up to have dark brown eyes and a generous mouth that would always be ready to break into a smile and ask her where Daddy was.

The farmhouse gate was firmly closed. There was a rope tied round the gate-post and the sign read, CAREFUL, CHILDREN PLAYING!

Jenni smiled. Some of her small nephews and nieces must be here. She climbed out of the car and opened the gate.

'Jenni, what a lovely surprise!'

Her sister, Gemma, came out of the back door, wiping her hands on a kitchen cloth. 'I'm just clearing away the lunch but. . .'

'I had a snack in hospital,' Jenni said quickly.

This was only partially true. She'd had a biscuit with her coffee but she simply hadn't felt like going into the canteen for lunch. There was the danger that she might bump into Carl and she didn't yet feel ready to see him again in an off-duty situation.

'Kate, Penny and Vicky are building a dam in the stream,' Gemma said. 'They shot off as soon as they'd finished their treacle pudding.'

'Where's Mum?' Jenni said, sitting down at the kitchen table and accepting the mug of tea that Gemma placed in front of her.

'She's gone on a day's outing with the WI. We came to stay for a week so I told Mum not to cancel any of her usual engagements.'

Gemma paused, her eyes searching Jenni's face. 'Are you OK, Jenni? You don't look your usual ebullient self.'

Jenni looked across at her sister and thought how predictable and organised Gemma's life seemed. Her fair hair was brushed back into a becoming chignon, not a strand out of place in spite of coping with lunch and her lively daughters. Would it help to confide in her big sister? She'd always been a tower of strength for Jenni when they were younger. It was worth a try.

'You know, there are only three years separating us, Gemma, but our lifestyles are so different. You had absolutely no qualms about giving up your teaching when you married Chris. You've totally submerged yourself in. . .'

'Now, hang on a minute, Jenni,' her sister broke in. 'If this is your soap-box speech about women maintaining their independence then. . .'

'It's not, Gemma!'

Jenni ran a hand through her hair distractedly as she tried to put her feelings into words. 'I'm so confused I don't know what to make of what's happening to me.'

'Don't tell me you've fallen in love!'

Gemma leaned back against her chair and smiled happily. 'Well, I never! My little sister has finally been swept off her feet. We all knew you wouldn't be able to hold out. Who's the lucky man?'

'Gemma, it's not like that! Oh, it's all so complicated. I mean, yes, I think I've fallen in love. . .but I don't want to be in love. I have to remain independent because this man. . .'

'Jenni, I know you've always said that you didn't want to be bossed around by any man. You used to say that it annoyed you the way Mum always gave in to Dad. And I remember you listening in when Chris and I were discussing the family holiday last year. I wanted to go to Cornwall and Chris wanted to go to France.'

'So you went to France, I remember,' Jenni said.

Gemma smiled. 'And you told me I should have

exerted my authority—got what I wanted for a change. But what you don't realise is that appearances can be deceptive in a marriage. Relationships aren't always what they seem on the surface. Only the couple involved know exactly what goes on inside that marriage. Women like me, whose men are strong and forceful, box clever.'

Jenni puckered her brow. 'Box clever? What do you mean?'

'We establish a partnership but, for the sake of the fragile male ego, we allow it to appear that our man is the boss. Now don't you think you could get it into your stubborn little head that a touch of compromise here and there is worth it for the wonderfully rewarding life of being married to the man you love?'

Jenni swallowed. 'Gemma, that's not really the problem any more. I think. . .I mean there might be a possibility that I would consider taking your advice. But, you see, this man. . .'

'Is he married?'

'No, he's not married. At least, not any more. And he doesn't want to be married ever again. He suffers from terminally itchy feet.'

Gemma nodded sagely, her eyes sympathetic.

'Ah, I see. Then you really do have a problem, Jenni. I won't pry. But if you need another chat I'm always willing to listen.'

'Thanks, Sis. I've got to get back. Flying visit. Give the girls my love. Tell them I'll come over again at the weekend.'

During the next few days Jenni mulled over Gemma's words and came to the conclusion that there wasn't much she could do about her relationship with Carl.

She had to go on pretending that she hadn't changed. Because she was sure that he hadn't! So ahead of her lay weeks of pretence before he finally went out of her life.

During the last week of July her period arrived again. She looked in the staff cloakroom mirror and told herself that she couldn't go through with another session of love-making with Carl. She couldn't allow herself to get completely carried away in his arms when it didn't mean a thing to him.

And the thought of bearing his child now disturbed her. If he wasn't going to be around she didn't want to be constantly reminded of him.

Safely ensconced in her office, she boiled the kettle and made a cafetière of coffee. The door opened. She looked up and drew in her breath.

'I thought I smelt coffee,' Carl said, nonchalantly, sinking down into a chair and sprawling his legs across the floor. 'I thought I'd have to make an appointment to find you. Why do I get the feeling you've been avoiding me?'

'I don't know what you mean.'

She handed him a cup of coffee, before sitting down at her desk.

'I've phoned twice and had a riveting conversation with your answerphone which patently lied when it promised me that Sister Dugdale would get back to me as soon as possible. I even thought of sending semaphore signals across the valley but. . .'

'Carl, I've been spending most of my off-duty time over in Riversdale with the family. It's school holidays and Mum is surrounded by grandchildren so she likes me to go and help her.'

He smiled. 'Which I'm sure you thoroughly enjoyed. Any babies there?'

'My brother Freddy's youngest is six months. I took him for a walk in his pram yesterday over the field path down to the stream.'

She paused. 'Carl, my period's arrived again and. . .'

His carefree expression changed to one of sympathy. 'You must be so disappointed. But, don't worry, we. . .'

'Carl, I don't know if we can go on like this.'

There! She'd said it and, amazingly, he didn't look in the least surprised. Perhaps he'd been expecting it.

'Look, if you think I'm getting fed up with. . .'

'No! No, I don't.'

She drew in her breath. How could she spell it out to him?

'Carl, that's not the problem,' she began carefully. 'It just seems to be going on a long time. And last time we were together. . .'

'Last time was wonderful!'

'Exactly! But this was an operation to conceive a baby—we never intended to get carried away like that.'

'But where was the harm? You enjoyed it, I enjoyed it. The next time. . .'

'Carl, I don't know if there should be a next time,' she said quietly.

He put down his coffee-cup and crossed the room. Reaching her desk, he put his arm around her shoulders.

'Jenni, I don't know what's worrying you, but I'd be really disappointed if we didn't get together again to try to make a baby for you. I know how much you want one and. . .'

'Yes, I really do want a baby,' she said quietly.

'Well, then, we mustn't stop trying. We must keep on until. . .'

'Until you go away,' she said, turning to look up at him.

His eyes flickered. 'We'll be successful before October. We'll. . .'

The door opened.

'What is it, Nurse?' Jenni snapped, before regaining her composure and feeling sorry for the young student nurse hovering on the threshold.

'Sorry to interrupt, Sister, but Staff Nurse sent me to tell you that Caroline Murgatroyd seems a bit funny this morning.'

'Funny?' Jenny was already on her feet. 'How do you mean, Nurse?'

'Well, Staff Nurse says Mrs Murgatroyd's a diabetic and she's becoming a bit delirious. Her sentences are all disjointed and half of what she says. . .'

Jenni shot out of the door, Carl hot on her heels. As they hurried along to the antenatal unit Jenni was reminding Carl of the details of this case.

'Caroline Murgatroyd has been a diabetic since she was a child. She's in her mid-twenties and expecting her first child, hopefully in eight weeks time, but I doubt we'll let her go to full term. We admitted her last week because her blood glucose level was too high and we've been unable to stabilise it.'

'And I remember that Caroline's latest uterine scan showed the foetus to be abnormally large. This isn't unusual with diabetic mothers. I think we'll have to do a Caesarean because I doubt the baby will pass through the mother's vagina when the time comes.'

Jenny nodded. They'd reached the patient's bedside. A worried Staff Nurse Penny Drew was holding Caroline's hand and leaning over her. Caroline was rolling around the bed, muttering incoherently.

'Caroline, can you hear me?' Jenni said.

Caroline stopped muttering for a few seconds and looked up at Jenni.

The patient closed her eyes. 'I'm very hot. . .and my head's splitting. How's my baby?'

'Baby's fine,' Carl said as he palpated Caroline's abdomen.

A laboratory messenger arrived with the latest blood glucose test result and Jenni passed it to Carl. He raised his eyebrows.

'I'm going to take you to Theatre, Caroline, and we'll get baby out today.'

'We'd hoped to carry on for another couple of weeks or so, hadn't we?' Jenni whispered to Carl.

He straightened up and went to the end of the bed. Jenni followed.

'It's a difficult decision to make,' he said quietly. 'But, weighing up all the facts, I don't think we can afford to hang about. If we allow Caroline to continue with the pregnancy the baby may die in the womb. Then, again, if I operate the baby may risk death from prematurity.'

'I think you're right to go ahead with a Caesarean section,' Jenni said. 'At least this baby is larger than normal at thirty-two weeks. I'll send a nurse from the prem unit to be on hand with an incubator as soon as you've got the baby out.'

'Thanks, Jenni.'

Within minutes Caroline had been taken to Theatre. Jenni carried on with her routine tasks while she waited for the outcome of the Caesarean.

An emergency patient arrived in the antenatal ward and Jenni paged Brian Hobbs, one of the housemen.

'Carl's in Theatre,' she told him as the fair-haired

young doctor hurried in through the swing doors, looking unusually worried. Jenni had found him to be a conscientious young doctor—keen to learn, theoretically sound—but still very inexperienced.

'This is Beth Johnson,' she told him. 'She's in considerable pain, her temperature is high and she's been sick.'

'How many weeks pregnant?' Brian Hobbs asked Jenni.

'Thirty. I've checked on the foetus and it's not showing any signs of distress. I've done a urine test and from the acidity and the distinctive odour I would say that Beth may be suffering from pyelonephritis.'

'That's a bacterial infection involving the ureter, renal pelvis and kidney, isn't it?' Dr Hobbs said.

'That's what I think it could be so I've sent off a specimen for analysis at the lab. The most common organism in these cases, as you probably know, is called the *Escherichia coli* so if that's what the lab decides is the cause of the problem then we've got our diagnosis. Would you like to examine Mrs Johnson, Dr Hobbs?'

'Of course.'

Jenni watched as Brian began to palpate their patient's abdomen. She'd nursed several cases of pyelonephritis and the outcome of her treatment had always been successful. She found herself wondering if this was the first case that Brian had ever seen. If so, he wouldn't be averse to a little help.

'As soon as the result comes back from the lab I'll let you know, Doctor. We can treat the bacteria involved with the appropriate antibiotics. Meanwhile, I'll make sure that Beth drinks large quantities of fluid. If she can't keep it down we'll have to put up a drip.'

Brian nodded sagely. 'I agree, Sister. I'll write up

the antibiotics for you as soon as we get the lab results.'

'Thanks, Doctor.'

Jenni was called away to the nurses' station to take a phone call. It was Carl, ringing from Theatre to say that he was keeping Caroline Murgatroyd in Recovery until her condition was more stable.

'And the baby?' she asked apprehensively.

'In the prem unit. A boy—two and a half kilos. Not bad for thirty-two weeks.'

'But is he OK? How are his lungs?'

'All the postnatal checks are good so far. Go and take a look for yourself when you have a minute to spare.'

'I will. Thanks, Carl.'

She put the phone back on its cradle. Staff Nurse Rona Phillips was coming through the swing doors, accompanying a new patient who was being admitted from Outpatients. Jenni said a few reassuring words to the patient, before assigning Staff Nurse Carol Thomas to take care of her.

There was no urgency about treatment for this new patient. When Carol had settled her in her bed Jenni would ask Brian Hobbs to take a case history.

Jenni made for the door, intent on examining the latest addition to the prem unit. It was such a relief to know that Carl had been right to operate when he did.

Rona Phillips caught up with her in the corridor. 'Haven't seen you for ages, Jenni. How's life treating you?'

'Fine, Rona.' Jenni put on her professional smile as she waited for the expected interrogation.

'A little bird told me you've been seeing a lot of the divine Carl,' Rona said.

'Which little bird was that?' Jenni asked, making a

valiant effort to keep the smile on her face as she quickened her step.

'Several little birds told me the same story, Jenni.'

'Then you must be utterly bored by it,' Jenni said, putting her hand on the door of the prem unit. 'Bye, Rona!'

As she went into the warm atmosphere of the prem unit Jenni was thinking that there was so much grapevine speculation about her relationship with Carl. Only the two of them knew the truth. And, since her conversation with Carl this morning, she wasn't even sure that she knew what the truth was!

The latest prem looked terribly vulnerable as he lay in his incubator, connected to continually bleeping monitoring wires.

'He's a good colour, Sister,' Nurse Judy Hickling observed.

Jenni was studying the monitor. 'Yes, he looks like a fighter to me.'

'He'll pull through, don't you think, Sister?'

Jenni heard the anxious tone of the young nurse and felt the need to reassure her.

'Baby Murgatroyd isn't out of the woods yet, but all the clinical signs indicate that he stands a very good chance of survival, Nurse.'

'What name is his mother going to give him, Sister?'

'We don't know yet. Mother's still in Recovery.'

Caroline Murgatroyd arrived back on Nightingale at the end of the afternoon. Jenni helped to settle her into bed, sponged her and put a clean nightdress on her.

'I've been admiring your wonderful baby son, Caroline. Any ideas for names?'

'Samuel, after his grandpa,' Caroline said drowsily, as she leaned against her pillows and went back to sleep.

Carl arrived at the nurses' station as Jenni handed over to Carol Thomas. She was due for an evening off tonight from six o'clock.

'As we've both got a free evening would you like to come back to my place?' he said as they walked down the corridor together.

'I'm absolutely whacked. I'm planning a quiet evening in and. . .'

'It's David's turn to cook tonight. You'll never know what you missed if you turn us both down.'

'Oh, David's at home tonight, is he?' she asked in an innocent voice. That put an altogether different complexion on the situation! 'I thought he was on nights.'

'No, this week he's on days.'

'Well, in that case I accept.'

Carl led as they drove in convoy over to the White House in Cragdale. The warmth of the summer day still lingered in the garden as Jenni parked behind Carl and climbed out of her car.

David came bounding down the steps, looking like an overgrown schoolboy in khaki shorts, bright red T-shirt and flip-flops.

'Great! You persuaded her, Dad! I knew you would.'

'Let me tell you, she wasn't a pushover. I had to practically fix a tow-rope to the bumper of her car.'

Jenni smiled. 'So my visit was planned, was it?'

'Certainly was!' David said. 'Dad was going to do his best to talk you into it, but he said you had a mind of your own and wouldn't take kindly to being hijacked.'

Carl reached up and ruffled his son's hair affectionately. 'You talk too much. What about the cold beer I ordered this morning?'

'In the fridge, sir. Go and sit in the garden. Everything's ready.'

Jenni followed Carl to a crazy-paved area in the centre of the rose garden and sat down on one of the rustic chairs that surrounded a large, circular table. Mopsy, the resident cat, strolled out from the bushes and climbed on Jenni's lap, purring contentedly.

Carl leaned across the table and took hold of Jenni's hand. She felt a sensual tingling of her skin where he was touching her. Had he any idea how difficult any physical contact with him was becoming?

'I'm glad you could come, Jenni. I meant to ask you this morning but you seemed understandably depressed because you weren't pregnant, and then we both got caught up in work. Don't let the situation get you down. You will get pregnant, I'm sure.'

She withdrew her hand, which felt as if it were on fire. 'I hope so.'

David arrived at the table with his father's beer, a glass of wine for Jenni and a glass of milk for himself.

'Going to the Coach and Horses later?' Jenni asked, pointing to the milk.

David grinned. 'How did you guess? Now, which would you prefer—fish and chips or fish and chips?'

Carl deliberated and agreed he'd take the dish of the day; Jenni followed suit.

It seemed perfectly natural to Jenni to be eating fish and chips in the middle of the rose garden, with the sun sinking lower in the sky and Mopsy waiting patiently for a morsel of fish at the end of the meal.

'That was really delicious, David,' she said, dropping a piece of fish for the waiting cat. 'How did you learn to make batter like that? Did your mother teach you?'

David laughed. 'You must be joking! Mum couldn't cook. In South Africa we had a cook and in the States we lived off take-aways or went out for meals.'

Jenni heard the impatient intake of Carl's breath and didn't dare to look at him.

David was continuing with his explanation.

'I worked in a restaurant in the summer vacation when I was sixteen. I was only supposed to wash up but it was so boring that I made a point of trying to learn what the cooks were doing. After a while they got an extra hand to do the washing-up and let me help with the cooking. Next time you come I'll cook you something really cordon bleu.'

'David wanted to treat you to the one and only Yorkshire dish in his repertoire,' Carl said, smiling.

Jenni was beginning to feel overwhelmed by the warm feeling of affection surrounding her. Carl and David were going to such trouble to ensure that she enjoyed herself. She felt as if she were part of their family and that was hard for her to take, knowing how transient this relationship was going to be.

'When would you like me to finish your drive, Jenni?' David asked. 'Dad said you've been out a lot lately, but I could finish it even if you weren't there. There's water from the garden tap. That's all I need.'

'Drop in any time,' Jenni said quickly, before she could change her mind. 'I've got a spare key somewhere in my bag... Here it is! Go into the house and help yourself to a glass of milk or whatever you fancy. There's a tin of home-made biscuits on top of the fridge.'

David smiled as he took the key. 'Thanks, Jenni.'

'Don't thank me,' she said quickly. 'You're the one who's doing me a favour.'

'Got to dash. Don't wait up, Dad. I may be late.' David was already sprinting over to his car.

Carl smiled. 'Drive carefully!'

Jenni leaned back in her chair and looked up at the darkening sky. 'I'm sure he will. He's a sensible boy.'

'He's a wonderful boy. I love him so much,' Carl said quietly.

Jenni heard the catch in his voice and her heart went out to him. 'Have you told David you're leaving Moortown at the end of October?'

He gave a deep sigh. 'I had to. If I hadn't somebody else would have done. And, anyway, the relentless march of time. . .'

'How did he take it?' she said hastily, unwilling to contemplate the fact that October was drawing ever nearer.

'He looked a bit shocked, then he pulled himself together and said. . .he said he'd coped without me all these years so there would be no problem. . . Oh, Jenni!'

He jumped to his feet and came round the table. She stood up as he put his arms around her and held her close. She told herself that it was comfort he was wanting, not passion. Reassurance from another human being.

'I should have been there when he was growing up. I missed all those years and now. . .'

He pulled himself away, still holding her by the hands, and looked down at her. 'I'm sorry, I shouldn't burden you with my problems.'

'I don't mind. Carl, you mustn't torture yourself. David has turned out to be an exceptional young man in spite of. . .in spite of everything that's happened to him.'

'He always tries to appear as if he hasn't got a care in the world. . .'

'As you do,' Jenni put in quietly. 'He keeps his problems to himself and he's as tough as old boots— like you!'

Carl gave a wry smile as he put his finger under her chin, tilting her face towards him. 'You've got us both sized up, haven't you?'

'Certainly have!'

She remained quite still, knowing that he was going to kiss her. . .wanting him to kiss her. . .anticipating the feel of his lips. . .

He bent his head slowly and his kiss was gentle at first, then more passionate. His tongue parted her lips and she melted against him, giving in to the waves of pleasure that swept over her.

Gently he released her from his arms.

'I've got to get back,' Jenni said quickly, trying to return to normality and not wanting Carl to see how moved she'd been.

He put an arm round her waist as he walked with her to the car.

'So, shall we set a date for our next operation?' he asked softly.

'In a couple of weeks,' Jenni said, before she could change her mind.

'So that's some time in the middle of August,' Carl agreed. 'And, Jenni, let's try to take the whole day off before the op. One of the reasons you haven't conceived might be because you're too tired at the end of a day in hospital. Let's have a whole day to ourselves and then you'll be refreshed and ready.'

She gave a little shiver of anticipation as the reality of what they were planning dawned upon her.

'Are you cold, Jenni?'

'I think I must be. I'd better get in the car,' she said quickly as she climbed in and started the engine. 'Goodnight, Carl.'

CHAPTER EIGHT

IT WAS the 'glorious twelfth' of August—the day when grouse shooting would begin up on the moors above Cragdale. Jenni lay in bed and wiggled her toes, luxuriating in the feeling of having absolutely nothing to do! Today she was going to be a lady of leisure and enjoy every last minute.

It hadn't been easy to arrange her off-duty to coincide with Carl's day off so she was going to make the most of it. Carl had suggested a picnic in Cornerdale, one of the more remote dales, and she'd readily gone along with that.

Looking out of the window, she saw that the sun was already high in the sky and was beaming down from a cloudless stretch of blue. Mustn't waste a second of this glorious day! Carl had invited himself for breakfast.

She showered and pulled on cotton shorts and a T-shirt, looked in the mirror and decided to wear a skirt. The shorts made her look too wildly available—which she wasn't! Well, not until this evening.

At the thought of the evening that would be the culmination of this day of pleasure she felt her pulse beginning to race. As Carl had said last time, there was no reason why they shouldn't enjoy being together. And that was exactly what she was going to do—throw caution to the wind. After all, if she was deliriously happy at the time of conception it might have a beneficial effect on her baby.

'Yes, I owe it to my baby to be relaxed and happy,'

she said out loud as she lifted croissants from the freezer and placed them under the grill.

Crunching tyres sounded on the drive. The door was wide open so she continued with her breakfast preparations.

'Mmm, something smells good,' Carl said, his lips brushing the side of her cheek. 'Croissants! Ooh la la! Very French.'

'If *Monsieur* would like to take breakfast at my pavement café perhaps he would be so kind as to carry out the cafetière.'

Jenni followed Carl into the garden with the croissants and apricot jam.

'What a perfect morning!' Carl said, pouring out the coffee before helping himself to a croissant from the tray on the garden table. 'David's gone to Scotland for a few days. His girlfriend's father has some kind of estate up there and David's been invited to a grouse shoot.'

'I didn't know he had a girlfriend.'

'Her name's Helen. He met her in London a couple of months ago, apparently, and she phoned him last week to say that she'd got herself a place in the nursing school here at Moortown. She invited him to go up to Scotland to meet her parents. He immediately arranged a few days off. Seems quite keen but, of course, he's very young.'

Jenni smiled. 'Same age you were when he was born. Still, I'm glad he's making lots of friends over here. It will be easier for him when you go away.'

'I've been thinking about that,' Carl said slowly, swallowing hard on a piece of croissant. 'If this cruise line directorship weren't such a fantastic job—the opening I've been waiting for—I would honestly consider. . .'

She held her breath as she waited for him to continue. He looked across the table, his eyes deeply troubled.

'But, then, again, Jenni. . .'

'Oh, you must stick to your plans,' Jenni cut in, trying desperately to hide her disappointment.

If Carl was having any doubts about changing his career plans then Jenni knew that it wouldn't work. Carl would never change! He might have been profoundly affected by the arrival of his son, but he still wanted to keep his freedom.

So, if she intended to enjoy the rest of her time with him, she must accept him for what he was—a totally independent character.

As she had been until Carl had come into her life and the joys of total independence had become less appealing.

'More coffee?' She picked up the cafetière.

'Yes, please,' he said absently. 'Tell me about Cornerdale. I've only read about it in the guide-books. It sounded so beautiful I thought it would be a good place to explore.'

'I went there a few times when I was a child. Difficult to get to from the road. You have to climb down a ravine beside a waterfall. Yes, it's very beautiful—very remote and peaceful.'

'Sounds just the sort of place to put us in the right mood for this evening,' he said, his tone giving nothing away.

She nodded. 'Yes, it will be very relaxing, apart from the waterfall descent and the return climb, of course.'

A brief expression of concern crossed his eyes. 'You won't find it too tiring?'

She smiled. 'Not half as tiring as spending the day on Nightingale. Come on, let's go!'

She put her rucksack beside Carl's in the boot of his car and they headed off over the moorland road towards the far dales. The sun's rays illuminated the bright gold of the gorse and the purple of the heather. Sheep cropped the dry grass at the side of the road. A rabbit scuttled across the road and hid in the bushes.

It was mid-morning by the time they reached Cornerdale. Carl parked the car on a wide grass verge, and they began their walk along the path that led to the waterfall. Reaching the top, Jenni looked down into the tumbling, cascading spray.

'This view never ceases to excite me,' Jenni said. 'It scares me too. My dad used to hold my hand when I was a child so that I wouldn't fall over.'

Carl held out his hand. 'Take mine, Jenni.'

She took his hand and they stood close together, while tiny droplets of water sprayed their faces.

'I can't hold onto your hand going down,' Jenni said. 'The rocky path's too narrow. Anyway, I'm a big girl now!'

Carl laughed. 'Come on, we're getting wet here.'

They laughed and joked as they scrambled down the path, sometimes slipping into each other, and Jenni found that she was quite deliberately holding on for longer than necessary. She was breathless when she reached the crystal-clear pool at the bottom.

'I'm so hot,' she said, pulling the T-shirt out of the waistband of her skirt in an attempt to cool her skin. 'When we were children Mum and Dad used to bring our swimming costumes and. . .'

'Now she tells me!' Carl said. 'Still, who needs a
swimsuit on a hot day like this? Come on, Jenni, don't
be coy! You'll enjoy the picnic so much better if we
cool down first.'

She hesitated. There was no one around to see them.

Carl had dumped his clothes on the grass, and was
already sprinting towards a large rock at the side of the
deep pool. She watched him pause for a moment on
the rock, before diving down and emerging seconds
later from the water.

'It's wonderful! Come on Jenni, what are you
waiting for?'

She stripped off and ran to a smaller rock, easing
herself gently into the water.

'Ouch! It's cold!'

Carl laughed. 'That's what you wanted, wasn't it?'

She swam out to the middle of the pool. He
came towards her. She trod water as they met in the
middle.

'Don't go near the place where the waterfall hits the
pool, Jenni,' Carl said. 'You're. . .you're very precious
to me. I wouldn't want anything to happen to you.'

Her heart seemed to make a little joyful somersault.
That was the nearest Carl had ever got to telling her
that he loved her—which of course he didn't! But she
could dream, couldn't she?

She turned over and lay on her back—quite motion-
less—staring up at the blue sky and dreaming that when
she climbed out of the pool Carl would take her in his
arms and tell her that he couldn't live without her. He
would. . .

He was right beside her. 'I've never been able to
float on the top of the water like that, Jenni.'

'My brothers used to say it was because I was full of

hot air,' she quipped as she tried to return to normality.

Carl laughed. 'Come on, race you to that rock!'

He reached the rock first and held out his hand to pull her out. The rock felt warm. They stretched out in the warm sunshine.

'Automatic drying machine,' Jenni said, desperately aware of Carl's naked thigh against hers.

He raised himself on one elbow and looked down at her. She caught her breath as she saw the look of tenderness in his eyes. He was reaching out to touch her face. He tilted his head and kissed her on the lips. She looked up at the leafy tree, shading them from the view of the shore. A larger rock beside them obscured their view of the path.

She felt as if they were on their own little desert island, far away from civilisation. A primitive, primeval desire was welling up inside her as Carl began to caress her breasts. Her skin was tingling with excitement and anticipation. He covered her body with his own. The exquisite contact sent ripples of sensation down her spine, and when the ultimate fulfilment came she cried out in ecstatic release.

Afterwards they lay back on the warm rock, their arms entwined around each other. Jenni closed her eyes in delicious contentment. This was no dream—this was reality and she was loving every moment of it.

'It's much better when we don't plan,' Carl said huskily, his lips against her hair.

'Perhaps this time we've been successful,' she said, turning to look at him. 'We could call off our planned operation for tonight.'

His eyes flickered. 'Do you want to call it off, Jenni?'

She smiled. 'No, do you?'

He pulled her into his arms. 'Absolutely not! I

think we should keep trying until we have positive
results.'

He held her hand as they negotiated the rocks back
to the grassy shoreline. Fully clothed, Jenni emptied the
contents of her rucksack on to the grass.

'Plastic plates, chicken sandwiches, fruit cake,
apples, home-made biscuits. . . That's about it.'

Carl was opening the wine he'd brought with him.
He handed her a stainless-steel cup.

'To our baby!' he said, raising his cup. 'Oops! Slip
of the tongue. I meant to say, to your baby!'

She raised her cup. How would he react if she told
him that she was seriously coming to the conclusion
that she wanted to share their baby?

A young couple, having threaded their way gingerly
down the path, were approaching the pool—sitting
down only yards away from them. Jenni knew that the
moment had passed. She couldn't change the rules of
their game. She had no idea how Carl would react but
it would be sure to spoil their tenuous relationship.

They explored the lower reaches of the river after
their picnic, before returning and clambering back up
the waterfall path and to the car.

The air was beginning to cool down as they sat in
Carl's garden, drinking tea and eating Jenni's home-
made biscuits. The whole of the evening stretched ahead
of them. Far from feeling satiated by their love-making,
Jenni found that she was anticipating being close to
Carl again.

A cool wind had started to blow up the valley.

'Let's go inside,' Carl said. 'We'll have supper in
the kitchen. Grilled bacon and scrambled eggs OK?'

She smiled. 'Lovely!' She was starving hungry again.
The outdoor life had given her a ravenous appetite.

But anything that Carl cooked tonight would taste delicious.

She set the kitchen table before rocking in her favourite chair, from where she could watch Carl as he scrambled the eggs.

He held both hands out across the table when they'd finished their meal.

He smiled, his eyes tender and full of affection. 'Let's go to bed and make sure we've made a baby.'

There was no mistaking the urgency in his voice. Jenni stood up, her body already feeling limp with anticipation. She looked at the array of dishes scattered around the kitchen.

'Don't even think about the washing-up,' he said huskily.

They climbed the stairs together, Carl's arm around her waist. Standing barefoot on the thick, lush pile of the bedroom carpet, they undressed each other. Carl swept her up into his arms and carried her over to the bed.

The first magical touch of Carl's lips sent Jenni reeling into an orbit of passionate sensations. The awareness of every nerve ending was heightened by his caresses as she lost herself completely in their love-making.

When she first opened her eyes she didn't know where she was. And then reality dawned upon her. A bedside light was casting a dim shadow on Carl, who was still asleep. Through the window she could see the moon. She sat up in bed to peer at the bedside clock. Two o'clock? They'd been in bed for hours!

Carl stirred beside her and put out his hand. 'Don't go, Jenni.'

'I'm not going anywhere in the middle of the night,' she said, snuggling against him.

'Stay for breakfast,' he said, still half-asleep. 'In fact, why don't you move in? Yes, why don't you, Jenni?'

He raised himself on his elbow and looked down at her, his eyes misty with sleep and fulfilled passion.

'Carl, in the cold light of day everything will look different. I'm not going to leave my own cottage to move into a temporary situation.'

He closed his eyes and let his head fall back against the pillow again. 'Why do you always have to be so independent?' he murmured sleepily. 'Well, it was worth a try. Goodnight, Jenni.'

In the morning she indulged herself by luxuriating in the huge antique bath, liberally doused with bath-foam. Carl was still asleep. She was sure he wouldn't even remember having asked her to come and live with him.

She'd picked up her pile of clothes from the bedroom carpet and brought them into the bathroom with her. It was essential that she got away early so she had time to dress properly over at her cottage.

Carl was stirring when she got back into the bedroom.

'Why are you dressed?' he asked. 'Come back to bed. It's only six o'clock.'

'I need to go home. Can't go to hospital, looking like this.'

He smiled. 'You look wonderful to me. Sort of. . .yes, definitely different. As if you'd spent the night making love.'

'I thought we were trying to make a baby,' she said lightly, while her pulse increased rapidly.

He gave her a rakish grin. 'You may have been trying for a baby—I was making love.'

She hesitated. Should she tell him that the feeling was mutual? No, it could spoil everything between them. The reason Carl was so relaxed with her was because she made no emotional demands on him.

'Got to go,' she said quickly. 'See you in hospital.'

For the first part of her morning on Nightingale Jenni spent the time getting to know the new patients who'd arrived on her day off. There were four new babies in the postnatal unit whose young mothers needed advice and help with breast-feeding.

After helping and encouraging them, Jenni went into the prem unit to check the condition of a tiny premature baby girl who'd arrived in the night. Staff Nurse Carol Thomas gave Jenni a full report on baby Tina's condition while Jenni checked the monitor for herself.

'It's worrying that Tina's still so cyanosed, isn't it?' Jenni said, noting the blue colour of the baby's skin. She turned as she heard the sound of the swing doors. Stay calm! she told herself when she saw it was Carl. It was so difficult to be strictly professional after spending the night in his arms.

'I'm worried about Tina's cyanosis, Dr Devine,' she said in a deliberately professional tone.

Carl checked the oxygen that was flowing into the incubator. 'I'll slightly increase the oxygen, Sister. How does baby Tina cope with feeding?'

'Not very well,' Jenni said. 'Staff Nurse tells me that Tina has difficulty with breathing when she's lifted out of the incubator.'

'Then she'd better stay in the incubator until her colour improves,' Carl said. 'Sister, I'd like you to pass a Jacques' catheter down into baby's stomach. We'll start two-hourly tube feeds. I'll write up a high-calorie formula. Any other problems on Nightingale?'

Jenni shook her head. Nightingale was running smoothly and there wasn't anything that Carl would be willing to do to ease her own problem!

CHAPTER NINE

THE test was positive! Jenni checked and rechecked the thin coloured line in the specimen jar. Yes, she was definitely pregnant!

She sat down on the edge of her bath and looked at herself in the mirror. She still looked the same, but inside a small foetus was going to develop into her baby—Carl's baby.

At the thought of Carl she felt the familiar rapid increase of her pulse rate. It was four weeks since that magical day when they'd made love by the river in Cornerdale. In the evening they'd made love at Carl's house and she'd lain in his arms until dawn.

So she really hadn't been too surprised when her period was late! For nearly two weeks she'd kept it to herself, not giving Carl any intimatation that she might be pregnant. And then, this morning, she'd used the pregnancy test kit and got the result she'd dreamed about.

She started to work out the dates. It was now mid-September. Her last period had started during the last week of July so her baby would arrive at the end of April or the beginning of May. A spring baby.

But where would Carl be in the spring? Somewhere on the high seas. She told herself that she wouldn't even think about it. She had to enjoy being with him for the next few weeks, and then let him go. She'd achieved what she'd set out to do. She was having Carl's baby!

Oh, she simply had to tell him the good news! She raced down the stairs and picked up the phone. A sleepy voice answered, 'Hello.'

'Carl, I'm pregnant!'

'Jenni, are you sure? Are you absolutely sure?'

He sounded wide awake now and his excitement matched her own.

'The test is positive. I've checked and rechecked. Carl, I'm going to have a baby!'

'Congratulations! I think we should celebrate. I have to go to Leeds today to a medical conference, but we could meet later. Will you be off duty this evening?'

'I'll make sure I am. It isn't every day you find out there's a baby on the way.'

'I'll pick you up about seven o'clock. And, Jenni. . .' he paused '. . .take care of yourself.'

'Of course I will.'

She put down the phone. It was obvious that he was thrilled with the news. And he really did care about her! But not enough to change his lifestyle. Carl Devine was a free spirit and nobody would ever succeed in taming him.

She found it hard to concentrate on her work during the day. Everything on Nightingale suddenly seemed so beautiful! The mothers were charming and the babies, although not without problems, seemed to conform to a new pattern. As she went about her duties she felt as if she were floating on air. She wanted to tell everybody that she was going to have a baby—but she didn't!

She hadn't yet worked out how she was going to handle the hospital grapevine. It was one thing to achieve her pregnancy, but quite another to announce it

to the world. Maybe she should wait until her condition
became obvious.

Staff Nurse Carol Thomas took over from Jenni at
six o'clock and she drove home to Cragdale. A quick
shower and a change of clothing and she was waiting
downstairs, longing for the sound of Carl's tyres on her
newly completed drive. As she heard the sound of an
engine slowing down in the road she flung open the
front door.

Carl pulled the car to a halt and switched off the
engine. As she saw him extricating his long legs from
the driving seat her heart was so full of love that she
felt as if it would burst. This wonderful man was the
father of her baby. If only she could tell him how much
she loved him!

He seemed to be walking more slowly than usual as
he came towards her. She was impatient to be close to
him. He stretched out his arms and she went into them.
He pulled her against him, and for a few moments
neither of them spoke. When—eventually—he released
her from his arms she saw that his eyes, besides holding
an infinitely tender expression, were moist.

'Well done, Jenni,' he whispered, his voice husky
with emotion.

She smiled happily. 'I can't take all the credit. You
played a very important part.'

He laughed and she saw that he was back on his
usual form again.

'I can honestly say it was a pleasure. I hope you're
not going to dump me now that you've achieved your
ambition.'

'Certainly not. We can still go on being friends
until. . .until you go away.' She was aware that her
voice was wavering.

'It's six weeks to the end of October. Do you think you can stand having me around for all that length of time?'

'It's going to be a strain but I'll make a valiant effort.'

'We'd better get a move on. I've booked seats at the theatre in Leeds.'

She picked up her shoulder-bag. 'What's on?'

'It's that new play that everybody's raving about— written by Moortown's very own playwright. I thought we should introduce the baby to a spot of culture early on in his life. I think it may be a bit highbrow but I hope baby's mother will enjoy it.'

'I'm so happy I'll enjoy it whatever it's like.'

He put his arm round her waist and guided her towards the car.

'I'm so proud of you, Jenni,' he said as he opened the passenger door. 'I'm trying not to be proprietorial with you, but it certainly does make a difference to the way I feel about you, knowing that you're carrying my baby.'

She leaned back against the leather of the seat and waited for Carl to start up the engine.

'In what way have your feelings changed?' she asked cautiously as he turned out into the road.

'I feel I want to put a protective shell around you so that you'll be safe when I'm not with you.'

'I'll be perfectly safe on my own,' she said quietly.

'I know you will. You're the most self-sufficient person I've ever met.'

'Apart from yourself,' she prompted.

He laughed. 'That goes without saying.'

'We're two of a kind, aren't we, Carl?'

He took a hand from the wheel and covered hers. The touch of his fingers sent shivers down her spine.

She stared out through the windscreen and told herself to live in the present. Today was all that mattered. She would cope without Carl. She would have to!

They arrived at the theatre minutes before curtain-up. Jenni relaxed against her seat in the darkened auditorium and tried to concentrate on the play, but her mind flitted constantly to thoughts of her baby. She clasped her hands over her abdomen, mentally visualising the tiny fertilised egg that was growing inside her.

On stage the drama was unfolding—something about a man who had to go away and leave his woman behind, and the woman was devastated by the separation. So, what's new? Jenni thought. Maybe she should think about writing a play.

'What do you think of the play so far?' Carl asked as they went into the bar at the interval.

She smiled. 'To be honest, I'm having difficulty concentrating.'

He laughed. 'To be honest, so am I. What can I get you? Orange juice? Lemonade? You'd better not have any alcohol. Not till the pregnancy is well established. Then the occasional glass of wine with food would be OK but. . .'

'Carl, I've been caring for expectant mums for the whole of my professional life.'

'Sorry! It's just that this baby is so special to me. I know I said it was going to be your baby and I won't back down on my promise, but I can't help taking an interest at this stage.'

She watched him go over to the bar. The room was packed with people but she felt as if they were the only two people there.

The second half of the play passed in much the same way. She was cocooned in her own little unreal world, and the events on the stage didn't concern her. The only thing that affected her—besides the warm, glowing feeling of the knowledge of the baby inside her—was Carl, sitting close beside her. He had taken hold of her hand and the touch of his fingers made her skin tingle with sensuous pleasure.

After the play Carl took her to a small Italian restaurant near the theatre, where the lasagne and green salad tasted unusually delicious.

'I feel as if I'm looking at the world through rose-coloured spectacles,' Jenni said, as they drove back to Cragdale.

'Perhaps you are,' he said quietly. 'Sooner or later, we'll have to come down to earth and sort out the practicalities of the situation.'

She took a deep breath. 'What do you mean?'

'Well, for instance, are you going to acknowledge the fact that I'm the baby's father?'

'That's up to you,' she said quickly. 'Would you like it to be known?'

'Of course—but not yet.'

Carl turned the car into Jenni's drive and switched off the engine. He followed her inside and sat at the kitchen table while she made coffee.

'Jenni, there's something I've been wanting to ask you all evening.'

She sat down opposite him and poured out the coffee, trying to remain calm as she heard the urgency in his voice. She looked across and saw the troubled expression in his eyes.

'I know we agreed that it was to be your baby. Now, I'm not going to change our agreement, but I'd really like to see this baby after it's born. May I call in to see it occasionally? I'm trying not to become attached to it but. . .'

'Of course you can see it. . .if that's what you want. But originally you said you didn't want to have anything to do with the end product.'

'I can't believe I said that. It sounds so callous now! But that was what you wanted me to say, wasn't it, Jenni?'

She nodded. 'Yes, that was the original agreement.'

His expression softened. 'You know, ever since David turned up I've found myself becoming more and more conscious of what I missed by not seeing him when he was growing up.'

She waited, hardly daring to breathe. Carl actually admitting that he was changing was incredible!

'But don't worry, Jenni, I won't interfere with your plans. You'll have sole charge of the baby.'

She swallowed hard. 'Let's not discuss it any more. I'm feeling tired, Carl. It's been a long day.'

He stood up. 'You'd better get some sleep. I'll see you in hospital tomorrow.'

He kissed her lightly on the lips. She walked to the door and watched as he drove away. Locking the door, she found herself wondering how she would cope with the emotional tension when Carl came to see the baby.

As she climbed the stairs she realised that some of her initial euphoria was evaporating. There were so many problems to be solved, and most of them concerned Carl!

She gave herself a split duty next day so that she could spend the afternoon in Riversdale with her mother. She needed to talk through some of her problems. Arriving

at the farmhouse, she was relieved to find that her
mother was alone for once.

'What a lovely surprise, Jenni!' Susan Dugdale said.
'How long can you stay?'

'I've got to be back on duty at five,' Jenni said,
sitting down in her favourite comfy armchair beside the
smouldering kitchen fire. 'I wanted to have a chat with
you about something very important.'

Her mother smiled as she picked up the teapot and
poured out two cups. 'Sounds intriguing.'

'I'm going to have a baby.'

Mrs Dugdale put down the teapot and stared at her
daughter. 'Did you say. . .?'

'I'm pregnant. Baby's due in April. Oh, don't worry,
Mum, it was all planned.'

'So you really want this baby? In that case, I'm
delighted for you, Jenni. I know how you love babies.
Well, who's the lucky father?'

'It's Carl Devine, the man I brought here at Easter
when he drove me back to hospital from Trish's and
Adam's wedding reception.'

'Oh, I'm so glad it's him! I took an instant liking to
the young man. But you've kept it all very quiet. Call
me old-fashioned but presumably you're going to get
married, or are you going to have one of these modern
arrangements where you simply live together? I really
think that in the baby's interest. . .'

'Mum, there's not going to be a wedding. Carl's
moving on to another job at the end of October. We
had an agreement—I wanted a baby, Carl agreed to
help me out and. . .'

'Help you out? Oh, Jenni! It all sounds so cold and
clinical. You must have felt something for Carl when
the two of you got together to make this baby.'

'I did,' Jenni said in a small voice. 'I fell in love with him.'

Her mother's eyes registered concern. 'Ah, I see. And how does he feel about you?'

'I don't know. He's the sort of man who doesn't wear his heart on his sleeve. He's had an awful lot of emotional trauma in his life and he doesn't like to show his feelings. But he's made it quite clear that he wants to stick by the original agreement. The only change he wants to make is to be allowed to see the baby occasionally.'

'Well, it's only natural he'd want to see his own flesh and blood. My feeling is that when he sees the baby he won't be able to tear himself away.'

'Oh, but he will! You don't know Carl. He's very good at controlling his emotions. His ex-wife left him and took their baby boy away with her. It wasn't possible to contact them so he had to learn to put his feelings on ice. He won't find it a problem to forget my baby when he's away from it.'

'Well, I'd like to meet him again and try to get to know him, Jenni. Why don't you bring him to supper one evening? Any evening, and the sooner the better.'

'I don't think he'll come if he thinks you're going to talk him into. . .'

'I'm not going to talk him into anything, Jenni, dear. I simply want to get to know the father of my next grandchild. I'll respect whatever the pair of you have decided about the future. But I honestly believe that a baby needs two parents.'

Her mother's words kept repeating themselves in her head as Jenni drove back to hospital. The whole idea of having a baby for herself had changed since she'd fallen in love with Carl.

Promptly at five she took the Nightingale reins from Staff Nurse Penny Drew. There had been an emergency admission during the afternoon.

'Dr Devine is with the new patient now, Sister. He was asking for you earlier.'

'Thanks, Staff. I'll go and see him.'

Jenni found Carl, fixing an IV cannula into the new patient's arm.

'Mrs Graham's lost a lot of blood,' Carl said quietly. 'I've grouped and cross-matched her. This is the first bottle. I'm going to take her down to Theatre in half an hour.'

'What are you planning to do?' Jenni said, scanning the notes and learning that their patient, Barbara Graham, aged forty-five, had suffered profuse vaginal bleeding for the past three or four weeks.

Carl drew Jenni on one side out of earshot of the patient.

'I've discussed it with Mrs Graham and her husband, who was here earlier. Understandably, she's very weak after the profuse bleeding. I can't think why she put up with it for so long without complaining. Her husband said she's one of these women who hates to make a fuss. She thought her doctor would tell her it was something she had to put up with at her time of life.'

'I suppose she thought, like so many women, that the menopause was all about suffering in silence,' Jenni said.

'This is one of those cases where a hysterectomy should put things right. That's what I've advised and

Mrs Graham has agreed. Consent form's been signed
so. . .'

He paused, his eyes narrowing as he looked down
at Jenni.

'You're not looking your usual self this evening. Not
tiring yourself, are you?'

'I'm fine. Stop fussing!'

'Can't help it,' he said, his voice husky.

She turned away. 'Go and get the theatre ready while
I deal with the pre-med.'

Jenni spent most of the evening in the postnatal unit
after Mrs Graham had been taken to Theatre. Looking
after the new babies was totally absorbing and she didn't
have time to think about her own problems.

As she returned to her office the swing doors opened
and Carl arrived, still in theatre greens. He held open
the doors to allow David to push Mrs Graham's trolley
through.

Jenni helped to transfer their unconscious patient into
her bed.

'Massive fibroids were the problem,' Carl said. 'They
were all over the lining of the womb so it was no
wonder she was bleeding so profusely. A hysterectomy
was the best solution.'

Jenni checked the flow of intravenous blood from
the drip, before assigning one of the nurses to special
the patient and report any changes in condition to her
immediately. She began to walk back towards the office.

'I've got to write up my report for the night staff,'
she told Carl.

'Any chance of a coffee?' he asked. 'David was just
saying how thirsty he is. He's actually off duty but he's
already worked half an hour extra.'

David smiled down at Jenni. 'I need a lift home with Dad because my car's in the local garage.'

'Again!' Carl said. 'We'll have to get you something more reliable.'

Jenni pushed open the door of her office. 'It'll have to be a quick coffee because the night staff will be here in a few minutes.'

She lifted the cafetière from the hot plate and poured out two cups of coffee and a glass of water for herself. She'd suddenly gone completely off coffee. Settling herself behind her desk, she picked up her pen.

'Could I have your car, Dad, when you go away in October?' David said.

Jenni put down her pen, rapidly losing her concentration.

'Well, that's a possibility,' Carl said, looking across at Jenni. 'I'd been thinking that I'd take it to run around in when I'm based at head office in London, but I've discovered that there's an initial six-month assignment in the Far East so I'd better leave it with you.'

'Thanks, Dad. That's great!'

'Would you like to come home for supper, Jenni?' Carl said quietly. 'If you go home by yourself you probably won't bother to cook.'

'Yes, do come for supper, Jenni,' David said eagerly. 'I'll do my chicken *suprême* for you. And Dad will open one of his special bottles of wine.'

Jenni's eyes met Carl's.

'I've bought some non-alcoholic grape juice for you, Jenni,' Carl said quickly.

'Why?' David asked.

Jenni was shaking her head at Carl. The door opened and explanations were postponed.

'Mrs Graham's coming round, Sister,' said Nurse Judy Hickling.

Jenni stood up. 'I'm coming, Nurse.' She turned to look at Carl and David. 'I can't make it till about nine.'

David smiled. 'That's fine.'

Carl followed Jenni over to their patient. Jenni removed the airway from Mrs Graham's mouth and asked how she was feeling. She was still a bit groggy but relieved to hear from Carl and Jenni that the operation had been a success. Carl wrote up the relevant medication on Mrs Graham's chart.

'See you later,' he whispered, before going down the ward to rejoin his son.

Jenni finished her report and handed over to the night staff.

It was dark when she went out into the car park and a cool wind was blowing down from the moors. The winters could be harsh amid these northern hills and Jenni wasn't looking forward to the onset of the cold weather.

It had been such a lovely summer. She knew that, in the future, whenever she thought about the summer when her baby was conceived she would remember nothing but sunshine.

Sunshine and laughter, she told herself. She mustn't get morbid because Carl was going away. She must remember the wonderful times they'd spent together, for the sake of her baby.

The three of them had supper in the kitchen. David had prepared a creamy mushroom sauce to pour over chicken breasts in a casserole. Fresh broccoli and creamed potatoes garnished the dish.

'Delicious!' Jenni said, putting her fork down on the

empty plate and taking a sip of her grape juice. 'Thanks, David. You certainly are a talented cook.'

'Coffee, Jenni?' David asked.

She hesitated. 'I've gone off coffee. What I'd really like is a glass of cold milk.'

David went over to the fridge.

'Are you going to tell me why you didn't have a glass of wine tonight?' he asked quietly.

Carl looked at Jenni, his eyes pleading. 'The secret will have to come out soon.'

She took a deep breath. 'I'm going to have a baby, David.'

David gave a howl of delight. 'That's fantastic! It's Dad's, isn't it?'

Jenni smiled. 'Of course. Carl's been the only man in my life this summer.'

'So when are you two going to get married?'

Jenni swallowed hard. 'What a conventional young man you are! Just because I'm having a baby, it doesn't mean that we have to get married. I'm going to carry on with my life; Carl's going to go off to work in the Far East and. . .'

'It's all perfectly civilised,' Carl cut in, sensing that Jenni was searching for words of explanation.

'Is it?' David said. 'Don't you think the baby would be happier in a normal family?'

'What's normal?' Carl asked quietly.

'Don't ask me,' David said, walking over to the door. 'I never knew what normal was when I was growing up.'

He paused and took a deep breath. 'Sorry, Jenni, I didn't mean to spoil the evening for you.'

'You didn't, David,' Jenni said. 'I can understand how you feel.'

'You can? I doubt it. Well, I hope you'll be very happy with your baby, Jenni. You must let me see my little half-brother some time. Dad, I'm going to my room to have an early night.'

As the door closed Carl came round the table and put his hand on Jenni's shoulder.

'I'm sorry, Jenni. I didn't think David would react like that.'

She stood up. 'How did you think he would react?'

He put his arms around her and held her close. 'I've never seen him like that before. It's as if I don't know my own son.'

'You don't,' she said quietly.

'I should have been with him when he was growing up,' he said, his voice catching with undisguised sadness. 'If only I could recapture those lost years I. . .'

He paused. She waited, holding her breath.

'But I can't turn the clock back,' he said quietly.

For a fleeting moment Jenni wondered if she dared ask him not to make the same mistake again. But she knew that even though Carl regretted the lost years he hadn't changed.

'I've got to get back,' she said, pulling herself away. 'It's been a long day.'

'Where did you go this afternoon?'

'Over to see my mum.'

'Did you tell her the good news?'

Jenni nodded. 'Carl, she's asked me to take you over for supper one evening. You don't have to go if you don't want to. I can easily make an excuse for you if. . .'

'I'd like to go for supper.'

'You would?'

'Does she know I'm the father?'

'I think that's why she wants to see you again.'

He smiled. 'I thought it might be. Well, it'll be a challenge. Is your father going to produce a shotgun and ask me to make an honest woman of you?'

'Don't worry. I've told them about our mutual agreement.'

'Well, that's a relief! You're not having second thoughts about the baby, are you, Jenni? You're still pleased to be pregnant, aren't you?'

'I'm ecstatic!' she replied. 'It's the most wonderful thing that's ever happened to me.'

'That's what I thought. But you seemed worried about something tonight. You'll find that small worries assume vast proportions during pregnancy, Jenni.'

She smiled. 'Carl, I have studied the subject, you know. I'm not a complete novice. So stop fussing!'

He pulled her close. 'You were always special to me, but now. . .'

She heard the catch in his voice and waited.

He bent his head and kissed her lightly, gently, tenderly, on the lips, before pulling away and looking down into her eyes.

'You'd better go home before I carry you upstairs to my bed.'

Deep down she felt the warm familiar stirrings of sensual arousal. There was nothing she would like better than to spend the night in Carl's bed.

'I expect you don't approve of making love to a pregnant woman, do you?'

His fingers caressed her cheek. 'Not in the very early stages before the pregnancy's well established.'

'And in the later stages you won't be here,' she said quietly.

His eyes held an enigmatic expression but she could see the sadness behind them.

'Don't remind me, Jenni.'

'Goodnight, Carl.'

She turned and walked towards the door. This was the nearest she'd ever got to telling him how she really felt about him and he hadn't risen to the bait. He hadn't reacted in the way she'd hoped. She wouldn't try it again.

He walked out to the car with her. A full moon was illuminating the Cragdale valley. She heard the sound of a lone lamb, bleating on the hillside, and the faint noise of the rushing river below them. Her final weeks with Carl were going to be all too poignant. She had to be strong to keep up her pretence of indifference.

Her eyes were moist with tears. She didn't dare to look at Carl before she climbed into her car and set off down the valley.

CHAPTER TEN

A COUPLE of weeks later, on the evening when Jenni was due to take Carl to her parents' farmhouse for supper, she left the ward as soon as she'd given her report to Staff Nurse Carol Thomas.

Arriving back at the cottage, she went up to her room and looked at the outfit she'd laid out on the bed that morning. Last year's winter suit—grey worsted cloth, narrow skirt. On second thoughts, she decided that the waistband would be too tight and she wanted to feel comfortable for the ordeal.

She was so afraid that it would be an ordeal. She'd been mad to agree to take Carl over! Her parents were broad-minded but they would still insist on what they thought was best for their daughter—and their grandchild.

She pulled out a woollen dirndl skirt with a loose elasticated waist. That would give her a chance to breathe. A single strand of her grandmother's pearls around her neck to fill the neckline of her cashmere sweater completed the outfit.

Outside on the drive she heard tyres crunching to a halt. Grabbing her duffle-coat, she ran down the stairs.

'Hey, take your time!' Carl said as she opened the door. 'You shouldn't fly down those stairs in your condition.'

'I'm very fit. I don't believe that pregnant women should pamper themselves.'

'I do!' He leaned forward and kissed her on the lips. 'Especially when it's my baby.'

'Come on, we mustn't be late for supper.'

'We'll take my car, Jenni.'

She climbed in and fastened her seat belt.

'Don't wear that belt too tight, Jenni. I'm going to drive carefully so that I don't have to make any jerky stops.'

'Oh, Carl! Anybody would think I was the only woman in the world to be expecting a baby.'

'You are, as far as I'm concerned.'

She looked out of the car window at the fleeting dry stone walls. Carl's new-found tenderness was even harder to take than their first heady experiences of passion together. It was hard to take because she was terribly aware of how she would miss it when he wasn't there.

Carl drove down the cobbled track to the back door of the farmhouse.

'That's my sister Gemma's car,' Jenni said, pointing out the large green station wagon. 'Mum's probably invited Gemma and her husband Chris for moral support.'

Carl grinned. 'That sounds ominous.'

'Don't worry. My sister will be charming with you even if she doesn't approve of what we're doing.'

Gemma opened the door. 'Jenni, darling! And you must be Carl. We've all heard so much about you. Do come in.'

'What did I tell you?' Jenni whispered to Carl as they followed Gemma along the stoneflagged passage to the kitchen.

Jenni effected the necessary introductions. Gemma's husband, Chris, a tall, fair-haired university lecturer in

blue denims and a corduroy shirt, shook hands
with Carl.

Jenni's father, George—tall, grey-haired, in a brown
tweed jacket and grey flannels—escorted Carl to a
fireside chair.

'We're having our drinks in here so that you can chat
to me while I finish the cooking,' Susan Dugdale said.
'What would you like, Carl? Whiskey? Gin. . .?'

Carl settled for a beer as he sat down by the fireside
next to Jenni's father.

'Jenni tells me you're going off to the Far East, Carl,'
George Dugdale said.

Jenni moved across to the fireside and perched on a
stool near Carl. Carl immediately stood up and insisted
that she took his chair, even fixing a cushion in the
small of her back. As Carl stood, leaning against the
mantelpiece, Jenni looked across at Gemma and saw
that she was smiling with approval. Jenni smiled back.

'Yes, there's a lot of travelling involved in the new
job,' Carl said.

'Sounds wonderful to me,' Gemma's husband, Chris,
said, clutching a pewter tankard of beer as he walked
over to join the fireside group. 'I'd love to leave the
wife and kids behind and sail away somewhere. It must
be great to be footloose and fancy-free.'

Carl gave Chris a broad smile. 'Oh, it is!'

'But what's this I hear about a baby on the way?'
Chris asked. 'Won't that make a difference?'

'Why should it?' Jenni said quickly. 'I was the one
who wanted the baby. Carl's got his own life to lead.'

'Sounds like a perfect arrangement to me,' Jenni's
mother said, her head down as she stirred the gravy.

Jenni shot a glance at her mother. She was grateful
for her support but she felt sure that it wasn't genuine.

Why did she have the feeling that her mother was up to something?

'Everything's ready so we can go through to the dining-room,' Susan Dugdale said. 'George, you can carry the roast lamb; Jenni, take this dish of potatoes; Gemma, lift the plates from the oven. . .'

Mrs Dugdale marshalled her troops with the expertise of a general. When they were all settled at the table the conversation resumed. Carl was quizzed about his previous experience of being a cruise line doctor. Jenni admired the way he kept everyone's interest with stories of some of the more exciting episodes that had happened to him.

Susan Dugdale, in particular, seemed enthralled by Carl's travel stories. To Jenni's relief, no further mention was made of the baby. It was a lengthy meal and finished with apple pie, followed by cheese. When Mrs Dugdale suggested coffee Jenni stood up and said that she and Carl would have to go.

'Got an early start in the operating theatre tomorrow,' Carl said, standing up and putting his hand on Jenni's shoulder.

'Well, you must come again when you're over here,' Susan Dugdale said to Carl, walking beside him down the passage towards the door.

Jenni turned at the door to give her mother a kiss.

'Is it working?' her mother whispered.

Jenni was mystified. 'Is what. . .?'

She looked out of the door to where Carl was diplomatically moving out of earshot towards the car.

'I was trying to give the impression that I couldn't care less about the fact that Carl's going away,' Susan Dugdale explained. 'With an independent man like that it's no use begging him to stay. He'll only run the other way. So I thought he might, perversely, decide to stay if it seemed as if we didn't care.'

'Mum, it's very sweet of you, but it won't make any difference what we do. Carl has a very determined mind of his own.'

'But it's perfectly obvious that he's very fond of you, Jenni. You can't just stand by and let him slip through your fingers.'

'I'm not going to plead with him to stay, if that's what you mean. He wouldn't be happy being chained up in a permanent relationship.'

'How do you know? Have you asked him?'

'No, of course I haven't! Look, Mum, I've got to go. Thanks for supper.'

'Keep me posted, Jenni.'

'I will.'

Jenni climbed in the car. Carl started the engine, turned round in the yard and drove out on to the road before he spoke.

'What was all that about?'

Jenni took a deep breath. 'Oh, my mum's not too happy about our plans.'

'I thought she seemed perfectly happy with the situation.'

'That's because you don't know her very well. She's pretending to go along with the situation but really she wants all the conventional trimmings for her daughter.'

'Such as?'

'Oh, you know, husband. . .'

'And what do you want?'

'Me? I'm perfectly happy with our arrangement,' she said lightly.

'No, you're not. . .and neither am I, Jenni.'

He pulled the car into a layby and switched off the

engine. His arm came across the back of the seat and she looked up, startled, into his eyes.

'Let's stop the pretence,' he said, his voice firm, no-nonsense. 'You're as good an actress as your mother and I've had enough of it. I love you, Jenni, and I want you to be my wife. I want to be around when our baby is born.'

Her heart started thumping rapidly. 'Carl, you don't know what you're saying. It wouldn't work. We're both too independent.'

'We could make it work. Answer me honestly, Jenni. Do you feel exactly the same about me as you did when we first started trying to make a baby?'

'No, of course not! We've grown. . .well, we've grown closer together. How could we not do when we've spent all the summer together? But when you go away. . .'

'Jenni, I'm not going away. All that talk about the job tonight was a façade. Last week I asked to be released from my proposed directorship of the cruise line.'

Jenni remained speechless as she stared up at Carl, her mouth widening in astonishment.

'Oh, don't worry, they said there were plenty of applicants to fill my shoes. Their second choice would jump at the chance to replace me, but they've asked me to reconsider. I have to give them my decision next week.'

'But, Carl, you said this was your career chance of a lifetime.'

'That was last April—before I got to know you.' He leaned across and took her into his arms. 'That was before I fell in love with you.'

He bent his head and kissed her, oh, so tenderly on the lips.

Shivers of dormant passion ran down her spine.

'Oh, Carl, I don't know what to say. I don't. . .'

'Don't say anything, except that you'll marry me,' he whispered huskily. 'If I can give up my independence so can you.'

She pulled herself away and leaned back against the seat.

'Even if I could give up my independence I'm not sure that you could. You've been influenced by everything people have said in the last couple of weeks. David gave you a rough time when we said we were going to live separate lives; my brother-in-law made disparaging remarks about you being footloose and fancy-free.'

'Chris's remarks were like water off a duck's back, but I admit I was hurt by the way David reacted. It made me realise that my family commitments were more important to me than an adventurous career. I want to stay here with you, Jenni; I want to be with you when our baby is born and. . .'

'Oh, Carl, I'd love to believe you,' Jenni said. 'I really would. But can a leopard change his spots?'

He smiled as he leaned across and put one finger under her chin, tilting her face upwards so that she could see the tenderness in his eyes.

'This is one leopard who's going to try,' he said quietly.

'Well, keep trying, Carl, but don't make any hasty decisions. The door's still open for your cruise line job, isn't it?'

'Oh, yes, the door's still open. You're the only one who can close it now, Jenni.'

'No! I won't be made responsible for something that should be your decision.'

He ran a hand through his dark hair. 'But there's no point in giving up the job if you won't marry me, Jenni.'

'Carl, I can't make an instant decision. You've got to give me some time. I never expected this to happen. I never believed you were the marrying kind. I still don't!'

'I didn't believe you were the marrying kind, either, until I sensed you were changing towards me. If I can change so can you.'

'I don't think either of us should change,' Jenni said carefully. 'I love you the way you are.'

'And I love you for your stubborn independence, but surely we can both reach a compromise.'

Jenni drew in her breath. 'I hope so. Take me home, Carl. I suddenly feel very tired.'

'You work too hard on Nightingale,' he said as he started up the engine. 'Have you had an antenatal check yet?'

'Yes, Simon Delaware has taken me under his wing.'

'And. . .?'

'And everything's fine.'

'And does he know I'm the father?'

'No. I didn't think you wanted people to know yet. Simon's very discreet. He doesn't ask awkward questions and he recognises that my pregnancy is still a secret.'

'But not for long. Jenni, I'm going to tell Simon it's my baby. I want him to know. . .and then, as soon as you agree, I want the whole world to know!'

He took one hand off the wheel and placed it over hers.

'And I want you to marry me, Jenni. How soon can I have your answer? I have to phone the cruise line by the middle of next week.'

'Come to supper next Tuesday, Carl, and I'll have made up my mind.'

During the next few days Jenni's thoughts revolved around Carl's proposal. She had to come to a decision. Much as she would like to take the proposal at face value, she knew that she had to be realistic about it. Marriage was a big step. Marriage was for life, as far as she was concerned. And life was a long time!

On the following Tuesday she was due for her first antenatal scan with Simon Delaware. He'd suggested to Jenni that as she was still keeping her pregnancy a secret he would ask his wife, Hannah, to assist him in his consulting-room instead of one of the nurses.

Jenni took an hour off from the ward, leaving Staff Nurse Carol Thomas in charge.

'I'll be in Outpatients with Simon Delaware, if you need to get in touch,' she told Carol.

Simon and Hannah were waiting for her.

'It's good of you to come and help, Hannah,' Jenni said as she went behind the screen to strip.

'I was delighted when Simon told me the good news, Jenni,' Hannah said. 'Will you still carry on with your career in hospital?'

'Of course.' Jenni emerged from behind the screen, dressed in a cotton gown, and climbed onto the examination couch. 'I'll take maternity leave, get myself a first-class nanny and return as soon as possible.'

Hannah began smoothing cream over Jenni's abdomen. 'Well, I wish you luck. Even with our wonderful, motherly, live-in housekeeper, I can still only manage to be a part-time doctor. Maybe when they're all older I'll be able to return full time.'

'Yes, but you've got three children to cope with.'

'Well, you're not planning on having an only one, are you, Jenni?'

The question took her off guard. 'I was before. . .' Her voice trailed away.

'Would it help if you told me, off the record, that Carl Devine is your baby's father, Jenni?' Simon Delaware said, his eyes twinkling.

Jenni smiled. 'Did Carl tell you?'

'He didn't have to,' Hannah put in. 'It was obvious all through the summer by the way you two looked at each other that you were madly in love. So, back to my original question. You're not planning an only one are you?'

Hannah turned on the scanning machine. Jenni turned her head so that she could see the monitor, while Hannah moved the scanner across her abdomen.

'Hannah, Carl's got his own life to lead. This was only meant to be a baby for me,' Jenni said, her eyes riveted to the screen.

'Look, there it is, Jenni,' Hannah said. 'Can you see the little flashing light from where you are? That's the little heart beating.'

Jenni swallowed hard. Her eyes were misting up. She couldn't see clearly. 'Is it my eyes, Hannah? Am I seeing double or are there two flashing lights?'

Simon leaned forward and peered at the screen. 'Jenni's right!' he said, excitedly. 'You've got twins in there.'

Jenni leaned back against the pillow and took a deep breath to steady her nerves. Her pulse was racing. Twins! How absolutely wonderful! A ready-made family!

Hannah was beaming all over her face. 'Well, that answers my question. Whatever you'd originally planned, your baby's not going to be an only one. But, with two babies to cope with, do you still think Carl should go off and leave you?'

'I don't think he should give up his new career for me,' Jenni said.

'He already has,' Simon put in quietly. 'We had a long discussion about it yesterday. He's already cancelled his cruise line appointment and I've offered him a permanent job on my firm. I'm delighted to have someone of Carl's calibre staying on as senior registrar.'

'But we were going to discuss the situation tonight,' Jenni said, swinging her legs off the examination couch.

Simon grinned. 'I know, he told me. I think he wanted to make sure that your answer to his important question was yes.'

'It seems that everybody knows what's going on,' Jenni said as she went behind the screen to get dressed.

'Jenni, there really isn't any point trying to keep it secret any longer,' Hannah said. 'Why don't you tell Carl, tonight, that you'll marry him and then we can all celebrate the wonderful news?'

'But it's not as easy as that, Hannah,' Jenni said, emerging from behind the screen as she fixed her white starched apron in place.

'There's nothing I'd like better than to be Carl's wife, but I can't help feeling that he's proposed for all the wrong reasons. He's thinking with his heart and not his head. He's been carried away by regrets that he missed out on his son David's upbringing and he doesn't want to make the same mistake twice.'

'Well, that makes sense to me,' Simon said slowly. 'Jenni, there's nothing wrong in thinking with your heart. Not where love is concerned. And, take it from me, you can be absolutely sure that Carl loves you. . .and always will.'

'If I could only be sure,' Jenni said quietly.

'You can't be sure of anything where love is concerned,' Hannah said gently. 'But it's a very precious commodity, so don't throw it all away, Jenni.'

'I'll try not to. . . Look, I'd better get back to the ward. I left Carol Thomas in charge and. . .'

'Are you sure you feel up to it, Jenni?' Simon said. 'As your obstetrician, I'd be more than happy to sign you off for the day and bring in a replacement sister. It's something of a shock to find out you're expecting twins.'

'Thanks, Simon, but I'm OK,' Jenni said.

Back on the ward she tried to concentrate, but the shattering news kept running through her mind. Two little babies were curled up inside her! As she helped with the feeds she hugged the news to herself.

What would Carl say when she told him about the babies this evening? But, even more important, what answer was she going to give him?

CHAPTER ELEVEN

'Simon said you had something important to tell me about the baby,' Carl said, as he faced Jenni across the table. 'He was very secretive about it. He said it was your place to tell me, not his. There's nothing wrong, is there?'

Jenni smiled. She'd kept the exciting news to herself for the first part of their evening together.

As she'd cooked supper she'd been terribly aware that Carl was watching her intently. At one point he'd sprung to open the oven door for her, saying that she must be careful not to burn herself. She'd laughingly told him that she wasn't a Dresden china doll.

Now, as she removed the lid from the chicken casserole dish, she knew that she couldn't wait another second to share the news. She put down her serving spoon and reached across the table to take Carl's hand. It felt comforting, reassuring, solid. . .

'Carl, we're going to have twins!'

'Darling!'

He was on his feet, tearing round the table to clasp her in his arms. 'That's wonderful!' He pulled her to her feet and kissed her tenderly on the lips.

His fingers brushed away a strand of hair from her forehead as he looked down at her, his eyes full of happiness.

'And do you know what was equally wonderful? It was the way you included me just now. You said *we* were going to have twins.'

She laughed. 'Well, we are, aren't we?'

'Jenni, suddenly I'm not hungry any more. Supper can wait.'

He took her hand and led her into the sitting-room, pulling her onto his lap as he settled himself in a fireside chair.

'Simon also told me to talk some sense into your pretty little head.'

'That's only because he wants to keep you here. He knows a good senior registrar when he sees one.'

Carl smiled. 'Oh, so Simon told you about my permanent appointment, did he? What else did he tell you?'

'He said you'd closed the door on your cruise line career. Carl, what makes you think you won't regret it?'

His arms tightened about her.

'I lay in bed the other night after we'd had supper at your parents' and I thought about the future—*our* future together. I tried to imagine what life would be like without you. . .and I simply couldn't get a picture. Without you, Jenni, there's no future for me.'

She heard the husky tone of his voice and her heart went out to him.

'Carl, are you sure your new feelings haven't got something to do with all this unaccustomed emotion? You've been used to living your own independent life, and suddenly you're plunged into a family situation. You're enjoying the novelty of being surrounded by family love and. . .'

'My life without you was sterile, Jenni. When we started going out together it took me a few weeks to realise what was happening to me.'

'And what *was* happening to you?' Jenni asked gently.

He put his head back against the chair. 'My feelings

and emotions were waking up after a long, long sleep. I'd deliberately put them on ice when David was taken away from me. I thought that if I lived life on an emotionally superficial plane I wouldn't get hurt any more. And then you came alone and I had to rethink everything.'

She leaned back against him and closed her eyes. 'I suppose, in a way, that was what was happening to me. I'd always thought I would steer clear of being emotionally involved with a man. I needed to keep my independence and I'd seen how bossy the men in my family could be with their wives. I wasn't going to put up with any of that.'

She felt Carl's kiss on her cheek and opened her eyes. He was smiling down at her with a fond expression.

'My dear little independent Jenni. What makes you think I won't start bossing you around if you marry me?'

'I haven't said I will marry you.'

'I know you haven't. You're deliberately keeping me waiting, but I'm living in hope. All I said was that if we were to marry wouldn't you be afraid that I might turn into a bossy husband? Isn't that what you believe happens to all husbands? They begin to enjoy the power they exert to control their wives?'

She smiled. 'You've hit the nail on the head, Carl. That's exactly what I used to believe. But I had a long chat with my sister, Gemma, and she put me right. I've got a strategy to deal with that sort of behaviour. . .should I ever get married. . .and should my husband ever try to boss me around.'

'Jenni, you really are the most infuriating woman!' Carl's eyes were twinkling as he pulled her against his chest. 'Whatever this strategy is, there's no need to start using it yet. I'm going to keep on asking you until you give in so, Jenni, what's your answer? Will you marry me?'

She smiled. 'Yes, I will.'

His kiss was light but infinitely tender as his lips brushed hers.

'I wasn't going to take no for an answer,' he whispered as he pulled her closer. 'Let's go to bed and make love. It's been so long since I've been close to you, Jenni.'

She pulled away and looked quizzically into his eyes. 'I didn't think you approved of making love in pregnancy, Doctor.'

He smiled. 'Only in the very early stages. This is a ten week pregnancy, well established. I'll be very gentle with you, Jenni.'

She smiled back at him. 'Carl, you don't have to sell the idea to me. If you knew how frustrated I've been in the last few weeks. It's a well-known fact that some women enjoy making love with their partners in pregnancy and—the way I'm feeling at this moment—I'm definitely one of them.'

He stood up, scooping her up into his arms as he carried her over to the staircase.

'You won't be able to carry me much longer,' Jenni said as they mounted the stairs, her arms threaded around Carl's neck. 'Once the twins start growing bigger it'll be impossible.'

'I'll hire a crane,' Carl said, pushing open the bedroom door with his knee. 'I'll have it installed on the landing and hoist you into my bed every evening.'

Very gently he laid her down on the bed and slowly undressed her, covering her with the duvet. When he slid in beside her she reached out eagerly to pull him against her.

Their love-making was deliberately slow, gentle and tender. Jenni felt as if she were a treasured flower that Carl was trying to keep in perfect condition. He didn't want to harm one small petal.

But the effect of his gentleness was to heighten all her senses to fever pitch. And as their bodies fused together she felt herself rising to an ecstatic climax.

Afterwards she lay in Carl's arms, her head on his shoulder, breathing rapidly as she revelled in the waves of sensual excitement that rippled over her body.

Carl raised himself on his elbow and looked down into her eyes. 'That was wonderful, darling. You're sure you're all right? I didn't tire you?'

She smiled. 'I'm fine! Never felt better. And I'm starving hungry.'

'Oh, my poor lamb! You've had no supper. Stay here and I'll bring it up on a tray.'

She didn't protest. It was nice to feel pampered! She lay back against the pillows, listening to Carl pottering about in the kitchen. Minutes later he returned with a large tray on which he'd placed two soup plates of chicken casserole and two glasses of wine.

'Special occasion—you can have a glass of wine, Jenni.'

'Well, thank you, Doctor,' she said, moving to one side to allow him to get back into bed. 'This is nice. How did you reheat the casserole?'

'In the microwave. I can cook, you know. I don't get David to do all the cooking. When you come to live with us. . .'

'So I'm coming to live with you, am I?' Jenni said, lifting one eyebrow.

'Well, of course you are!'

'It's not a foregone conclusion,' Jenni said, swallowing a mouthful of chicken. 'I may want to stay here.'

Carl gave her a wry grin. 'Are we about to have our first matrimonial row?'

Jenni laughed. 'No, I was just testing your reaction. I love this cottage but we'll need a bigger place when the twins arrive.'

'That's what I thought. Now, we can start house-hunting or we can make our home in my White House. The estate agent phoned me last week to say that the people who own it have decided to sell. They've rented a place in Florida and want to buy it as soon as they sell their house.'

'But that's excellent! It's a lovely house. We could turn the dressing-room next to the master bedroom into a nursery and. . .'

'And I'll have to mend all the walls around the garden so that the twins don't run out on to the road. David will help me.'

'How's David going to react to all this?' Jenni said.

'Shall we go and find out?' Carl asked.

'What, now?'

'Why not? I'm so excited I'll never be able to sleep unless you're with me, Jenni. And I really don't like the thought of you living alone in your condition. Pack a suitcase with a few essentials and move in tonight. I can help you sort out the cottage over the next few weeks. You can put it on the market as soon as. . .'

'Hold on a minute! This is my home we're discussing. I love this place.'

'Well, you can keep it on, if you like,' Carl said, pulling a wry face. 'Don't let me influence you.'

Jenni smiled. 'No, it doesn't make sense to have two houses. I was just testing again.'

He grinned. 'That's what I thought. It's the secret strategy your sister told you about, isn't it?'

Jenni laughed. 'How did you guess? I'm boxing clever.'

'You're what?'

'You're only a man. You wouldn't understand.'

She put down her plate on the bedside table. 'Would you get my suitcase down from the top of the wardrobe, please? I'm going to pack some clothes.'

An hour later they arrived at the White House. All the lights in the house were on and loud music drifted out to greet them.

'David's most definitely in!' Carl said as he switched off the engine.

Jenni felt a sudden wave of apprehension. Supposing David didn't want a stepmother moving into his father's house. She looked up at Carl as he opened the passenger door for her.

'Carl, what shall we do if David doesn't like the new arrangement?'

Carl put his hands on her shoulders and the expression in his eyes was deeply tender.

'Jenni, I can honestly say that David adores you already. He couldn't understand why we wanted to lead separate lives. He's constantly been telling me what a mistake it would be.'

He put his arm round her as they climbed the stone steps to the front door. David opened the door. Carl scooped Jenni up into his arms.

'I'd better carry Jenni over the threshold now,' Carl said. 'If I wait until after the wedding she may be too heavy.'

'Wedding?' David said. 'Did you say wedding?'

Carl put Jenni down, gently, in the hall.

'The wicked stepmother arrives,' Jenni said, watching closely to judge David's reaction.

'Oh, that's wonderful!' David threw his arms around Jenni and lifted her off her feet.

'Hey, be careful of your little brothers,' Carl said laughingly.

'Might be sisters,' Jenni said.

'Or one of each.'

David was looking puzzled. 'You mean. . .?'

Carl gave him a broad smile. 'We're expecting twins!'

David sat down on the hall chest. 'Wow!'

Jenni smiled. 'You look shell-shocked, David.'

David ran a hand through his dark hair. 'I am. It's the most wonderful news! When's the wedding?'

Carl looked at Jenni. 'I'd like it as soon as possible. How about you, Jenni?'

'I know you're dying for me to make an honest man of you so, shall we say, in a month's time?'

'A month's time? Why so long?'

'Because there's so much to be organised. My mum will. . .' Jenni paused. 'I've just remembered. I haven't told my mum yet. I must give her a call now. She'll need a whole month to help me sort out the bridesmaids and what everybody's wearing and. . .'

'So, shall we say the end of October?' Carl said.

Jenni smiled. 'How about early November?'

They were married in Cragdale Church on a crisp November morning. White hoar-frost covered the ground as Jenni, holding on to her father's arm so that she wouldn't slip, walked carefully up the path. Her mother's dressmaker had lined the cream silk dress to make it warm, but Jenni was so happy that she wouldn't have felt the cold anyway.

Inside the porch she could feel the welcoming heat from the radiators, gushing out to meet her.

'You're not nervous, are you, Jenni?' her father whispered.

She smiled. 'Not a bit.'

'I am,' he said.

'You'll be fine. Hold on to me, Dad.' She turned to look at the six little bridesmaids behind her. 'Everybody OK?'

Seven-year-old Kate, Gemma's eldest daughter and the oldest of the bridesmaids, smiled up at her aunt. 'Don't worry. I've got them all under control.'

Jenni checked the six little heads. They were all there. It had been difficult to assemble the group this morning over at her parents' house but now all the little girls seemed ready to attempt the walk down the aisle in their long ivory-white dresses.

It had been important to include all her nieces. She wouldn't have dared to leave anyone out! Her brother Gavin's daughter, four-year-old Francesca, was holding on to Kate's hand. Kate's two sisters—Penny, aged six, and Vicky a year younger—walked close behind. The final pair were Freddy's daughters—Felicity and Naomi, aged five and four.

The organist had begun playing the music Jenni and Carl had chosen together. It was time to go in. She took a deep breath and smoothed her hand over the front of her gown. The loose folds concealed the slight roundness of her abdomen and the generous cut of the gown wasn't constricting in any way.

She moved into the church, holding lightly to her father's arm. Her friends, relatives and medical colleagues were straining to catch a glimpse of her as she walked past each pew and she turned to smile at them. Everyone had been so happy when she and Carl had announced that they were going to be married.

She was drawing close to the front of the church.

The bridegroom and best man were waiting in front of the altar. From behind the two men looked like brothers, rather than father and son—both tall, their dark hair with that distinctive hint of gold shining in the flickering candlelight that augmented the pale illumination of the rays of the sun, slanting through the stained glass windows.

David couldn't resist turning round to look at his stepmother. He smiled affectionately, his eyes showing how happy he was.

Carl waited until Jenni was actually standing beside him before he turned to look at her. She saw her own love mirrored in his eyes. His smile was infinitely tender.

As the service proceeded she found herself longing for the moment when she would be alone with Carl again. Tonight. . .

David had produced the rings from his pocket. Well, that was a relief! Carl had been afraid that his son might lose them.

The two rings had been specially made by a local craftsman.

Carl slipped the smooth gold band on Jenni's finger and she put the other ring on his.

'I now pronounce you man and wife. . .' the vicar was saying.

Jenni looked up at Carl. Were they really married now?

The service had gone so quickly. He was smiling

down at her. His kiss was spontaneous and gentle, a natural reaction. Later, when they were alone, they would have all the time in the world to show their love.

'Happy?' Carl whispered as they walked out through the porch to face the battery of cameras.

She squeezed his arm. 'What do you think?'

'And how are Tweedledum and Tweedledee?'

'I'm sure I felt them playing football just now.'

'Not at fifteen weeks, Jenni.'

'My babies are very advanced for their age, Doctor.'

'*Our* babies!' Carl said.

'Smile for the camera, please!' the photographers called.

'You'll have to wait a moment,' Carl said, as he took Jenni in his arms and kissed her.

Cameras flashed to capture the precious moment.

EPILOGUE

CAMERAS clicked in the hot June sunshine as the christening party emerged through the Cragdale Church porch. Jenni was carrying baby Richard and beside her Carl cradled baby Alice. Behind the proud parents came relatives, friends and medical colleagues.

'It seems only yesterday that we were standing here having the wedding photographs taken,' Carl said to Jenni in between smiles to the cameras.

Jenni laughed. 'You didn't have to carry these two around all through the winter. It seems like years to me!'

'Jenni, dear, how many of these people are going back to your house?' Susan Dugdale whispered anxiously.

Jenni smiled. 'All of them. Now, don't worry, Mum. Everything's under control. Maureen's supervising the caterers and David and his girlfriend, Helen, have already left the church and gone home to give a hand.'

Mrs Dugdale's worried expression softened. 'I'd forgotten that Maureen works in the house full-time now. Are you sure there's nothing I can do to help, Jenni?'

'Would you like to hold Alice for a little while?'

'I'd love to!'

The proud grandmother took the tiny dark-haired baby in her arms.

'She's got your eyes, Jenni, but that's definitely Carl's hair. See how the gold threads are glinting in the sunlight?'

'And Richard's a chip off the old block too,' Jenni

said, looking down lovingly at her dark-haired baby boy. 'He's even got Carl's chin. Look at the determined way he's pushed it forward.'

Carl laughed. 'He's a boy who'll know his own mind, except when it comes to dealing with women—and then he'll probably be a pushover, like his father.'

'Are you complaining?' Jenni whispered.

'Would I dare?' he whispered back, his eyes expressively tender as he looked down at his wife.

Gemma came hurrying across the grass to ask if she could hold baby Richard.

'As the proud godmother I feel I deserve a cuddle. Looking at you two with your gorgeous babies, I'm beginning to feel quite broody again. It would be nice for the girls to have a baby brother.'

Jenni laughed. 'Have you told Chris?'

Gemma gave her a conspiratorial smile. 'Not yet. I'm waiting for the right moment to discuss it and then I'm going to make Chris think it was his idea.'

'So this time next year, Gemma, we'll all be gathered here at the church for another christening.'

'If I get my way,' Gemma said.

'Which you will!' Jenni said, shielding her eyes from the sun to watch a couple of cars leaving in the direction of the White House.

'Carl, we'd better go home and greet our guests,' Jenni said.

With the twins securely fastened into their special baby safety chairs in the back of the new family-sized car, they set off back to the White House.

Mopsy, the cat, strolled across the drive, waiting for Carl and Jenni to climb out and stroke her.

'Just you wait until Richard and Alice start playing

in the garden,' Carl said to Mopsy. 'You won't have
such a peaceful, pampered life then.'

Jenni laughed. 'Neither will I.'

Maureen, their former cleaning lady—now turned
full-time daily housekeeper—came running out onto
the front steps.

'Oh, Mrs Devine, I'm so glad you're here. The caterers are insisting I tell them the exact number of guests
and. . .'

'Somewhere between seventy and eighty but I can't
be sure,' Jenni said. 'We've picked up a few more in
the church. I'd better go and pacify them before I feed
the babies.'

'There was no need for the caterers to worry that there
wouldn't be enough food,' Jenni said as she surveyed
the remains of the garden buffet that had been carried
through to the kitchen at the end of the party.

'Look at all these chicken drumsticks! There's lots
of salad and even some salmon. I'll freeze some of it,
and I ought to start packing up portions of the christening cake to send to. . .'

'Leave it, Jenni!' Carl said, putting his arm round
her waist. 'There's another day tomorrow. Come and
sit in the garden. It's the most perfect evening. David's
taken Helen back to the nurses' home, Maureen's gone
home and the twins are asleep. We've got the place to
ourselves.'

Gently he drew her away from the table and out
through the kitchen door into the garden. Jenni looked
up at the open windows of their bedroom.

'Are you sure we'll hear the twins if they cry?'

'Jenni, the amount of noise those two can make will

be heard down by the river. Stop worrying. I'll keep checking on them.'

They sat down on the garden seat by the wrought-iron table. Carl took his arm from Jenni's shoulder and reached into the middle of one of the rose bushes.

'Here's something I prepared earlier,' he said, pulling out an ice-bucket—complete with champagne bottle. 'And if I'm not mistaken. . .yes, the glasses are still here.'

Jenni smiled. 'Is this a private party or can anyone join in?'

'By invitation only, and the list is now closed. So it's just the two of us. And the toast is to Richard and Alice!'

Jenni raised her glass. 'Not forgetting David and Helen!'

'To David and Helen,' Carl said. 'Tell me honestly, don't you think those two are a bit young to be going out together all the time?'

'David's nineteen, Helen's eighteen. You were only seventeen when you were married.'

'And look what a disaster that was! That's what I mean. I'd like David to have lots of girlfriends before he settles down. Play the field a bit!'

'Play the field!' Jenni repeated, pretending to be shocked.

Carl gave her a rakish grin. 'You know what I mean. Then, when he's sown a few wild oats, he can settle down with a mature, interesting. . .'

'Is that why you settled for me? Because I'm mature and interesting?' Jenni asked, pulling a wry face.

Carl put down his glass on the table and drew her into his arms. 'I didn't choose you for your maturity or your brilliant brain. You just happened to be the most perfect woman for me. I couldn't believe how lucky I was. . .and still am.'

'Even after all these long months of marriage,' Jenni smiled. 'I can't believe it's all worked out so wonderfully. You know, Carl, I was trying to think about my work on Nightingale the other day and I seem to have lost the urge to go back.'

She stirred in his arms and looked out across the valley to where the sun was dipping below the skyline of the hill behind her old cottage.

A young couple were living in the cottage now. She found herself wondering if they could possibly be as happy as she and Carl were. The sun disappeared, but an orange glow still lingered over the moors.

'Jenni, you don't have to go back to Nightingale if you don't want to,' Carl said gently. 'It's your decision.'

'I know. I thought I would be raring to get back to the hospital. It used to be my life, but now I've got Richard and Alice I feel so complete here at home. I don't want to leave them with somebody else. I want to be here when they start mixed feeding; I want to help them take their first steps. If I'm not here I might miss part of their growing up.'

'You might,' Carl said, his voice husky with emotion. He'd known that Jenni would feel like this from the moment she'd clutched at his hand as the twins were being born.

'So I'm planning to stay home until they're much bigger. The new temporary Sister on Nightingale is excellent. I know she'd love to step permanently into my shoes. Maybe when the twins start school. . .'

'Maybe when the twins start school they may have a younger brother or sister,' Carl said, his eyes twinkling.

Jenni smiled. 'Who knows?'

Carl put his head on one side, cupping a hand to his ear. 'Was that the twins?'

'I can't hear anything.'

'I think we should go in and check.'

'You said you would go, Carl.'

'So I did. But I need you with me for what I have in mind, Jenni.'

She laughed. 'I simply can't guess what that is.'

His arms tightened around her. 'Then I'll have to give you a clue. . .'

ARE YOU A FAN
OF MILLS & BOON®
MEDICAL ROMANCES™?

If YOU are a regular United Kingdom buyer of Mills & Boon's Medical Romances you might like to tell us your opinion of the books we publish to help us in publishing the books *you* like.

Mills & Boon have a Reader Panel of Medical Romance readers. Each person on the panel receives a questionnaire every third month asking her for *her* opinion of the books she has read in the past three months. All people who send in their replies will have a chance of winning a FREE year's supply of Medical Romances—48 books in all. If YOU would like to be considered for inclusion on the Panel please give us details about yourself below. All postage will be free. Younger readers are particularly welcome.

Year of birth............................Month ....

Age at completion of full-time education ....

Single ☐   Married ☐   Widowed ☐   Divorced ☐

Your name (print please) ....

Address...

....

.... Postcode ....

**THANK YOU! PLEASE PUT IN ENVELOPE AND POST TO
MILLS & BOON READER PANEL, FREEPOST SF195
PO BOX 152, SHEFFIELD S11 8TE**

DISCOVER

S THE —
ECRETS WITHIN

*Riveting and unforgettable -
the Australian saga of the decade!*

*For Tamara Vandelier, the final reckoning with
her mother is long overdue. Now she has
returned to the family's vineyard estate and
embarked on a destructive course that, in a
final, fatal clash, will reveal the secrets within....*

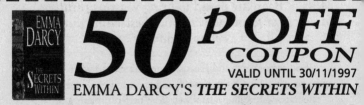

9 904170 180504

0472 00166